No Country for Cold Men

Demi Adeyemi

Matador
9 Priory Business Park,
Wistow Road, Kibworth Beauchamp,
Leicestershire. LE8 0RX
Tel: (+44) 116 279 2299
Fax: (+44) 116 279 2277
Email: books@troubador.co.uk
Web: www.troubador.co.uk/matador

ISBN 9781788037761

British Library Cataloguing in Publication Data.
A catalogue record for this book is available from the British Library.

Printed by CPI Ltd, Croydon, UK
Typeset in 10.5pt Minion Pro by Troubador Publishing Ltd, Leicester, UK

Matador is an imprint of Troubador Publishing Ltd

MIX
Paper from
responsible sources
FSC
www.fsc.org   FSC® C013604

To God. To my parents who I have put through so much.
To a wonderful family, both by blood and bond.
To everyone who believed so much in me,
even when I could not believe in myself.
Thank you.

1

This is not the beginning of the story, but sometimes the beginning is not what is important, it is its effect that we must pay attention to.

After what seemed like a forever of unyielding agony and incessant torture, he emerged. Slowly his light was born out of her darkness with blood coating him like a lamb lost in a thicket of branches. In a world full of people, the only reality for the other was listening to their mutual cry. Cries which could not even be heard as floods of the harshest rain poured down, completely muffling whatever was going on in that room, the appearance of which could only be described as basic and the primeval. Perhaps there was thunder, or perhaps it was simply the sound of the rain punching against the corrugated iron sheets that accompanied the disastrous chorus of sounds. Nevertheless it all proved to be soothing once his mother had taken the role of a father by relieving him of their uniting umbilical cord and nursed him to a peaceful sleep. She gazed at him, barely a burden upon her chest yet carrying such a heavy load upon his head; a head lined with wispy silvery strings, the day to her coarse and fragile night. She, like many of those in the deme to which she belonged, had no formal education other than that of the land, yet she knew that this would be the last time that they would be together for her charge was too great not to be worthy of the ultimate penalty.

Time seemed altogether absent from that room. Where there had been two bodies, there now was one. Life stood at her feet and death at her head. She had not made any attempt to tidy the blood that ruptured from between her legs due to the complications of his birth. The stains of the lifeblood, now saturated the more by the blood from the single slit to her throat. She had already heard the crescendo of the harrowing music of Death but another had ensured that their dance would be much sooner than was necessary. For this, she was grateful to her assassin for she too longed to be put to sleep.

After she had been put down, he tore it from the corpse and, making sure to conceal every inch of its skin, he candidly left the scene to his shadow-coloured car. Just as he had been trained never to question an order, he knew that despite the concealment of night, even if the eyes of neighbours did see him, their minds and mouths did not. Even beyond the choking grip of fear on the people, he was well aware that they would similarly justify her death if they knew of what she had given birth to; a defiance of natural order, an abomination that has forever been abhorred by their ancestors. As he drove away dark in the night, heading north towards the capital, he who was so used to committing the most heinous of crimes at the beck of his Fathers without even as much as a sesame seed of emotion really felt as though he had done her a favour, sparing her the hue of her humiliation. It lay in the back only comforted by the fact that it was still perfumed with her blood, completely unaware that the darkness it rode into now would not be dispelled even by the hottest sunlight. Worst of all, it lay unaware that its mother's final sentiments were thoughts deliberating whether or not she loved or despised her child.

2

The whole world revolved around Africa and the whole of Africa revolved around its ancient acclamation of the elders and tradition of Presbyterianism, which had officially become politicised, the extent of which was reflected by the geography of the continent. Rather than the out-dated practice of dividing the land into countries, which was believed to be an excuse for promoting individuality, Africa had been divided into zones, 20 to be exact, all arranged roughly concentrically around Capital which is where the five Fathers rule from. The zones were socially engineered to ensure a unity that could not be broken and to preserve the fundamental principles of respect and order. There were 5 demes: the Uppers, the Ones, the Middles, the Twos and the Lowers. Society operated whereby the Uppers and the Ones were the demes with any social standing and mobility and so their zones where the ones closest to Capital, with the Uppers slightly arching above the Ones because of their prestigious family names. The Middles, who lived further out, were characterised as being workingmen and so when they were of age, they would travel out to the superior zones in search of work, usually performing menial jobs to render whatever services were required. Unlike the top three demes, Twos are considered second-rate citizens and are not permitted access to work in or enter superior zones and so primarily turned to agriculture in order to make a living for themselves. Despite not being a people highly regarded, they are invaluable because of the vital role they play in what they bring to the table. Lowers however were regarded as nothing and so their zones were situated at the extremities of the continent. The extent of their nothingness is shown by the fact that of the four zones which each deme is allocated, two of the Lower zones, albeit the two largest zones, function as 'Wastelands' where criminals and enemies of the Capital are banished to.

The Fathers constitute of an elder from each deme who is theoretically supposed to have the best interest of his people at heart, but more often than not, the man chosen to be a Father is not the one who would fight on behalf of his people but would fight to be in the graces of the 'Father of All'; the Father from the deme of the Uppers, for by controlling that deme, he has the ultimate power.

Funke had made the journey, like many others from her zone, to try and find work. It was a journey she was forced to make a little sooner than she expected. Her father had been working in an Upper zone as a taxi driver but one day, after kissing his young son, his daughter and wife goodbye as he headed to work in the morning as per usual, when Funke heard the clock strike for midnight, in anticipation of his return she squeezed her eyes firmly as she routinely did, awaiting his goodnight kiss. However, her excitement began to fade and in its place, a sickening worry slowly emerged. In all fifteen years her father had never been late. Even her brother who had been fast asleep beside her in their bed began to jerk uncharacteristically. Eventually she fell asleep, expecting to see her father the following morning, but he never came back.

Funke's mother had been a seamstress in a One zone but a couple of weeks after the disappearance of her husband, she left her sewing and got a job as a nanny in an Upper zone because of the pay, but it was a residential position. As a result, Funke and her brother Folusho were moved to their mother's sister's house, which was just a few streets down from their house. The arrangement was supposed to be temporary, she would send money every month for their upkeep and once they had any news about their father, then she would return. But the hope of any news and the likelihood of her return diminished as the days and months passed, but surely enough, the money came.

The first six months with her aunt were fine, she looked after her brother and cousins, did whatever her aunt asked of her, still attended school and saw her friends; it wasn't ideal but they were okay. She still shared a bed with her brother, this acted as a comfort to her. After six months. at midnight one night, when she had just finished her usual prayer for her parents and was finally settling into sleep, she heard the door begin to open and watched her uncle silently make his way to her. Despite being slightly annoyed, she was ready to do whatever task he needed her for, after all he was her uncle and as a guest in his house she couldn't afford to be perceived as ungrateful or disrespectful, even at her inconvenience and at such a late hour. She realised two things that night; firstly, how naive she had been, and secondly, what alcohol smelled like. That wouldn't be his last visit.

Whatever time after that, her aunt must have realised because their relationship became more and more blunt until she sat Funke down one morning and told her that things were going slowly with her mother and so she needed to go and find work in one of the superior zones. She had gone to the extent of handing Funke an envelope with all necessary documents and work permits required for her work in the superior zones, all already filled in and approved, and even insisted that she leave that same day so that she can start looking for work as early as the next day. With what little she had, Funke packed her bag and by noon, she was already well on her way walking northwards towards the border. She had watched her parents cross the border several times although she herself had never crossed, but knew exactly what form was necessary at what stage, and more importantly, that it was essential for her to leave her true identity here buried deep in the ground with the assurance it would still be here safe when she returned. She left, stripped of every and all emotion because in the world she was about to cross in to, she does not exist, not because she doesn't live or breathe as the people on the other side do, but because her life is not as meaningful as theirs. So with rather mixed emotions, without the opportunity to say goodbye to her brother, she was signed, sealed and stamped into a complete unknown.

The car finally arrived, sailing smoothly through the narrow jungle of symmetrical tall trees on either side shrouding the neat road that led up to the gates of the Aso Rock Hill, the headquarters of the entire continent. The gothic gates opened and the car drifted, sleek like a bullet. As it was making its way not hastily but with purpose towards the stately building, through the breaking light of the wee hours, a man could be seen walking simultaneously down the grand steps equally focused on the car. He was obviously a man of high distinction, if his pace and posture didn't already dictate this, his attire definitely did.He was dressed in a baby blue buba and sokoto, draped with a matching agbada, the weight of which he carried with an unmatchable flare, crowned with his deeper blue fila and black oriental style shoes which looked as fierce as whatever animal they were made from. Finally his carved wooden walking stick with some sort of token adornment and deafening black sunglasses, one old the other new, echoed his exclusivity. He watched the car park and the assassin coolly step out; his full black suit, black shirt and skinny black tie still perfectly pinned made it difficult to determine where machine ended and man began. He fully prostrated in front of the man who was still making his way down the steps and said with his face still firmly facing the ground, "Good morning Father."

"Musa," The man paused in acknowledgement of his words. He spoke with absolute inscrutability "I trust it was all well taken care of."

"Yes Father, as always."

"So where is it?"

"I have it back in the car."

The Father hesitated, this time slowed with contemplation. "Bring it. I want to see."

The assassin quickly produced the baby and held it out to the Father but the Father made no attempt to collect it, but intensely inspected it, the severity of his gaze cloaked by his sunglasses of steel. The assassin had cleaned up the baby and wrapped it in a fresh blanket, glistening almost as much as the skin of the baby. This was not his first time of making an illegitimate child disappear.

"So what would you like for me to do with it Father, the usual?"

"No." he replied, remembering himself. "This one is different. I have to wash my hands completely clean of it therefore I cannot be soiled by its blood. Take it to the North Wasteland. I have made arrangements there." After this he took off his sunglasses, and staring deeply at the sleeping child, finally revealed the horror that gripped him at this. Then just as suddenly, he snapped his sunglasses back on and his frozen posterior was immediately restored. He slowly turned his back to the baby and began his ascent back into the building, sounding his walking stick at each step.

"When you deliver the package, the rest of the money will be wired to you."

Just as effortlessly, the car rode out of the gates.

3

I often dream about just treading lightly on newly sprung grass, or lying on a riverbank with the sun beating my back, carelessly placing my hand in the water to feel the current push through. Or maybe about getting lost in a forest somewhere and feeling the dew drop off high branches and plucking fresh fruit from the trees. When I was younger, I used to tell aunty Gloria of my dreams but she would always say the same thing, "Adekanmi you know that you are not allowed to go outside, the sun is not good for your skin. Don't have this type of dream again." But I did have these dreams again, in fact, I longed for them. When Officer would come back from work at the prison, the three of us would watch television together. Sometimes there would be children playing or people riding bicycles or hawking goods on the streets and I just wanted to experience that for myself. One time, when I was 14, I actually did go outside. Aunty Gloria had taken the bus to the nearest zone to buy foodstuff and Officer was at work. Aunty Gloria had set me some house chores and some reading exercises to get on with as she always did, but that day I decided to ignore that, I put on one of Officer's work shoes because the only shoes I had were rubber slippers, then left our little house. I walked and walked and walked in no particular direction for what felt like hours and enjoyed every second of it. I noticed that Wasteland was as rough as its name because the ground was so uneven and the foliage was so wild and scary. Fortunately for me I didn't come into contact with any animals, because based on the books that I had read with Aunty Gloria this looked like the kind of place to inhabit wild dogs, baboons and even snakes. The atmosphere was quite dry and hot which must have meant that it was harmattan season, Aunty Gloria taught me about geography too. She taught me about photosynthesis because one time, she noticed how I would always stare at the plants growing outside behind our house from the kitchen window. There had been no plants behind the house before but then they suddenly began to blossom when I turned about 10. Aunty Gloria then decided to cut one of the nicer looking plants, one with a purple flower, and she put it in a cup which she had already filled with some mud and she told me that it was my responsibility to look after that little flower. I cried so hard the day that flower died.

When I was outside, I saw many purple flowers like my flower, in fact I saw many other flowers too, red, orange, even white, but mostly just green. I tried to pick one of the flowers to take back home to grow but that flower had thorns which really hurt my hands so I just left it alone. Aunty Gloria had often warned me that the Wasteland was a very dangerous place, so I walked really slowly around, partly so I could take it all in but more importantly, because I can't see very well. When we would watch television at home, I would have to sit right in front of the TV because otherwise, I wouldn't be able to make out anything on the screen at all. Likewise, when I'm reading with Aunty Gloria, I would have to hold the book literally in front of my face to the extent where she would tease that I was trying to kiss the lovely girls in the story. I was enjoying myself so much on my little adventure that I didn't feel the need to go back home until I noticed that my skin was extremely hot and extremely uncomfortable. As I was making my return home, I remembered all the stories I had read of children lost in the forest laying out breadcrumbs and thread to help them find their way. I started feeling a little jealous because I couldn't remember how to get back and just as I started to panic, I felt a big heavy hand fall on my right shoulder. My alarm was quickly displaced with relief because it was Officer. Before a sheepish smile could even appear on my face, he whisked me home.

The minute we got home, he drew out his belt. The anger, the rage in his face, I had seen nothing like it. He looked like he was about to burst and sharp iron nails would fly scattering from the eruption. Officer is a man of extraordinary height and extraordinary build and the manner in which he came down on me was of epic proportion. With every strike of the belt, he would scream "Did anyone see you?" Of course no one saw me, no one lives here. The only other people that live here are the other prison officers and they live in prison quarters in or around the prison. Officer is allowed to live further out because he is the senior officer. Obviously I didn't say all this then because everyone knows that when you are getting beat, talking makes it worse.

When he was done, I apologised and went to get ready for bed. I wasn't hungry. All I could think about was why it was so bad for people to see me. What is wrong with me? As if Aunty Gloria could read my mind, later that night, she came into my room to rub Aloe Vera gel straight from the plant on my burnt skin and said that the reason why it is important that no one must ever see me is because if they did see me, they might think that her and officer had committed a crime, they would think that they had stolen me and that I was not their child. They would then take me away from them and all three of us would be punished. I didn't say anything in response to this but it made sense. I didn't want anything bad to ever happen to Aunty Gloria so I never left the house again. Though I didn't regret my adventure.

On my eighteenth birthday, Officer sat me down and said, "Adekanmi, now that you are 18, you cannot sit in the house all day. It is time for you to work. I have gotten you a job at the prison. You will be in charge of censoring all the letters that have been sent to the prisoners since your Aunty has taught you to read and write well. Anything that is threatening, radical or even remotely political must be burnt. I will personally train you for this position so that you properly understand what is acceptable and what isn't. Because this is a prison job, you will be required to live in prison quarters, but I believe that you are ready to handle the independence. You will move in next week, a room is ready for you. Happy birthday."

As you can imagine, I was so thrilled at this news, the opportunity to have a life outside of the house, to meet people sounded so surreal. Unfortunately the reality of what was in store for me was nothing like what I expected.

"Officer, why am I not staying with the other prison workers? Is this not a cell you have placed me in?"

"Adekanmi, you already know you are different to the others. You are educated and you are younger than they are. I don't want them to give you any trouble at all so it is best if you just stay by yourself."

"But is there not a house I can live in by myself, does is have to be a cell? How can I stay in a cell when I am not a criminal sir?"

"Adekanmi don't think about this place as a cell. Normal cells have bars to strip the prisoners of their privacy. You have a fortified door so no one will ever disturb you. Plus this entire wing is empty and will remain empty for as long as you're here. This whole wing belongs to you and you are allowed to wander around and act as you wish. If there is ever anything you want or need, it will be brought to you here. Remember, this is a prison, it is not safe for a young person to wander around by himself or herself. This is also where you will do your work. The letters will be brought to you in the afternoons and you are expected to be done censoring them by dinnertime. You will have no work on the weekends and your aunty has offered to spend every Sunday afternoon with you if you would like that. If for any reason you feel the need to leave the wing, you would have to seek permission from me before doing so. I hope that this is all clear."

And it was clear. I was trapped again, but this time I didn't mind so much because at least it was a change and I was ready for it.

Now I have been living in this wing for the past three years and I cant really complain.I actually quite enjoy my job, although

I have never met any of the prisoners, I know so much about them. Yusuf's daughter Latifah is getting married in three months time and she hopes that he will be out in time to walk her down the aisle. Taiwo's twin Kehinde is in hospital in need of a kidney transplant but there is no money to perform the surgery and a match has not been found yet. Tega's birthday is tomorrow and his daughter Blessing always makes him a card every year although she hasn't seen him since she was four. The truth is, there is really not that much work for me to do because only a handful of the prisoners get letters regularly. When I read the letters, sometimes I like to pretend that I am the person the letter is addressed to; that my wife misses me and my rent is due and my sister lost her job. I like to pretend that I have a life outside of these walls and that I have a family who loves me and can't wait to see me. For me, the best part of my week is when Aunty Gloria visits me. She always prepares a lunch for us to share and we talk and laugh about how grumpy Officer has been that week and how we are all getting old. We talk about travelling a lot, one time she brought a map and we were telling each other of the places we would go. Aunty Gloria always made extra snacks for me to keep around and brought a book for me to read that week to discuss the following week. I have an entire room where I keep all these books, it is easily my favourite part of the wing because whenever I feel lonely, I just go there and I can hear us discussing about Titus Andronicus and Oliver Twist and Hercules and Christopher Robin. Aunty Gloria really is the only person who visits me here. I still haven't met any of the other prison workers. Someone brings my meals here three times a day but they place it on a tray on the ground and knock three times and then leave. Officer says that I must wait ten

4

Aunty Gloria hasn't come to see me for three weeks now. When she didn't come the first time, I asked Officer and he told me that she was sick. This was very strange and I became extremely worried because I had never known Aunty Gloria to be sick before. When she didn't come for the second and third week I knew something was wrong. She had never not come to see me before and if she was so sick why didn't Officer stay at home to look after her. I missed her. I started sleeping in my library just to feel her presence but I really needed to be with her. She was the only person to ever show love to me. I started writing notes to her and giving them to Officer to deliver to her. At first I was writing about how much I wanted to see her and that I hoped that she would get better soon, but after a while, it didn't feel sincere anymore so I resulted to writing my opinion on the books that I had recently read. When I had exhausted that list I started writing about the books that I knew she loved, and then the books that I knew she hated. I didn't care, I just had to keep writing to her. I needed to keep her in my life somehow. Everyday I would give Officer her letter and everyday he would give me this look as if he wanted to steal the hope in my eyes and replace it for the grief in his. Every time I went to him I would look for a sign that things were getting better but he continued to look more and more miserable as the days went by.

Today's letter was about Frankenstein. The story were Victor Frankenstein creates a Creature but then refuses to acknowledge it and love it because in his eyes, and in the eyes of everyone that meets the Creature, the Creature is just a hideous monster not capable of being loved. Aunty Gloria loved this book. She said that everything has beauty inside, and that it was important to look past the superficial. I didn't like it.

"Officer, please make sure she gets this." As he took the letter from me and opened his drawer to place it in, I noticed something, the drawer was full of letters- my letters.

"What is this?" I brought them out "What is the meaning of this? Why wouldn't you give her my letters?" I could feel the tears welling up in my eyes as my voice began to quaver.

"Adekanmi, I can explain."

"What do you mean?"

"Adekanmi, I-"

"No, tell me. What happened?"

"She's dead"

At that moment everything began to fail me. My legs gave in and I fell hard to the floor, almost like the ground had disappeared beneath my feet, my heart gave in and I wasn't sure if I was conscious or not, my mouth dried up and my words ceased, my ears were ringing with those two words deafeningly audible. I watched the blood drain from the extremities of my body and my skin went from colourless to blue.

"She's dead." he repeated, this time, almost like an echo, as if he was telling himself also for the first time, like he didn't quite believe it.

"She knew she was dying, she made me promise not to tell you. I didn't even know how to tell myself. I asked her to go to the hospital, I begged her. She refused. She knew we couldn't afford it. My wife is gone and I don't even know what took her."

"No." I wanted to ask questions, like what did she say, how did she feel, did she ask for me. But all that could come out was "No. No. No."

"We buried her last week Thursday."

"No."

"We buried her at the churchyard of St Peter's in the Two zone about an hour southeast of here. She was friends with some of the ladies who used to sell cassava at the market. They helped me make the arrangements because ordinarily, we lowers aren't even allowed to be documented talk less of being buried in a Two zone. I'm sorry."

"I need to see here."

"Adekanmi, I-"

"I need to see her."

The room was silent. I had never spoken to Officer like this before but I didn't care.

"Ok. We will leave tonight."

I'm by myself now, lying in my bed, stiffened by anxiety.I don't know what is causing my heart to race more, the fact that Aunty Gloria is dead or the fact that I am not only leaving this prison tonight, I am going to a different zone. In my three years here, I've never as much as stepped out of the wing. I mean, I know I can, but there has just never been any need.I have food, I have entertainment, I have work, I have company- had, I had company. It is weird to think that I wont see her anymore. She is actually the only woman I've ever known. I have only ever known two people in my life and she was one of them. I have lost half of my world. One time, when I was younger, I asked her "Aunty Gloria, why don't I call you and Officer Mummy and Daddy like other people do on TV? Don't we live together? Are we not a family?" She said that we are a family, we are just a different type of family, that's all. I never quite understood what that meant, perhaps only Upper and One families called their parents mummy and daddy. There were no other Lower children like me to ask what they called their parents so it never really bothered me. She did all the things a mummy was supposed to do for me so it didn't matter anyway; she was still my mummy even if I couldn't call her that. But now she is gone. I wanted to just fall asleep and see her in my dreams but the pain in my heart was too much, to the extent that I feared that if I ever slept again, I would only have serious nightmares.

In the time that I spent thinking about Aunty Gloria, night soon came and I heard the familiar echoey jingle of Officer unlocking the door of the wing.

"Here, take this" he threw me a bag with another set of his uniform neatly folded inside. "Put it on."
I quickly got changed and just as we were about to step out into

the night, he stopped me and bent down to the ground, as if looking for something he had placed there. He then stood up and took me completely by surprise when he started rubbing mud from the ground all over my face and hands. I didn't ask why such bizarre action was necessary because I knew that the night was going to be filled with many more strange experiences, and if this was what I needed to do to be able to be with Aunty Gloria again, then so be it. He then removed his duty cap from his head and carefully placed it on mine, concealing every bit of my blond afro. I remember how Aunty Gloria used to smile whenever I wore that cap as a boy. I would feel so proud when I'd strut around the living room, I just wanted to be like Officer. One time, Officer even saw me in the hat and he just crossed his arms and was leaning in the doorway with a little grin on his face while he told me to stop being a silly boy. That was a good day.

We step out of the door and all I can see is blackness. All the prison lights are off and I feel just as empty being on the outside of these walls as I felt when I was within them. I think about what is was like the day I came here, It was about 1:30 in the afternoon, I remember because when I asked Officer why no one was around, he said that it was because they had all gone to lunch and we had already had lunch at home before we came. I remember noticing all the barbed wire fences and the sirens enclosing this place and feeling a bit overwhelmed, but then I saw the giant fields and felt excited again, the hope that I had for freedom was restored. Little did I know that I would never set foot on that field.

We walk all the way to Officer's car and he sits in the driver's seat and beckons me to sit in the front next to him. He puts the key into the ignition but before he starts the car, he turns to me and says, "Adekanmi, listen. This is very important. Whenever we come into contact with someone, you must look down at your shoes and not say a single word and not look up until I say you can. Do you understand?"

"Yes sir."

We drive to the front of the prison and I hear Officer mutter a few words to the guard on duty, something about cheap liquor and needing to go to the hospital. I wasn't really paying attention, I was too scared to focus on anything other than my shoes, and just like that, we were off.

The drive to this Two zone felt like forever. Whenever something from outside would catch my eye, the car would be jolted by another bump in the road and I would lose myself. But it was amazing. There was not much activity in the Wasteland so I felt so free as the speed of the car was allowing the hot breeze to hit my face so heavily. Just like that we were at the border and I once again was busy admiring my shoes. I heard officer laugh with the men and then he showed them his badge and explained that we were on official business. We were granted access and we soon sped away. I had never crossed borders before and the difference between this Two zone and Wasteland was as clear as day. The fields here were clearly cultivated, with tidy crops and bountiful vegetation. There were no rotten or fallen trees here. Even the roads were not as bumpy. However, perhaps the biggest distinction of all was the fact that despite the hour, there were people around. I could see people working on the land, people sitting down, people talking in pairs, people carrying heavy objects, people everywhere, not too many, but enough. It was amazing. They didn't see us though, or at least they didn't act like they saw us. I guess they were all used to seeing other people so they didn't care too much.

Officer drove for about 30 more minutes and as he was driving, I noticed all sorts of things; a florist, a bakery, a small church, a butcher, even a barbershop. The barbershop made me remember aunty Gloria because it made me think about how she would get so upset whenever Officer would try to cut my hair. She said that I was Samson and that it was wrong for anyone to cut my golden crown of curls. He would just huff and leave us alone. She used to take so much pride in my hair. She loved to wash my hair for me and sing old songs whilst doing it. As soon as my hair was long enough, she started cornrowing it and doing all manner of styles to it. Officer would be disgusted but he could never fight her on it. I think she wanted a little girl to raise. Nowadays I just tie my hair in a ponytail. It still makes Aunty Gloria happy.

We finally arrive at St Peter's and the sun is about to rise.

"We don't have much time" Officer says and he comes out of the car and starts walking to the back of the church building. I quickly follow him, trying to take in all the death around me. He keeps walking and walking until he reaches the spot where Aunty Gloria was buried. I was surprised to see that her grave didn't have a gravestone, in fact not many of the graves did. Officer said that it is because tombstones are expensive and Twos and Lowers don't have that kind of money. That the few that did have gravestones probably were people who were well-liked by the community enough for them to raise money to pay for it. When we got there, Officer got on his knees, buried his head in the ground and silently began to cry. I was so moved by this because I had never seen Officer get emotional before. I quickly followed suite and know who you are. There was an order from Capital for you to live with us. Who am I to refuse Capital? I don't know anything about you, I was just following orders."

"Leave" my head was ringing. I wasn't even sure if this conversation was taking place in my mind or in real life.

"You didn't even have a name when you came. You didn't have anything. We gave you everything. She gave you her life, I warned her, I begged her not to love you too much, that we were only doing this as a job. But for her, you were the answer to her prayers. She loved you. I am pretty sure that she died because of you, because she could only see you once a week and that killed her."

"Leave. Leave. Leave."

"I didn't even want to send you to that prison, I didn't want to separate you two, for her sake. I could see how much she needed you. But I didn't have a choice. I had to lock you away. I was ordered to. But I'm tired of obeying these stupid orders. These orders killed my wife. All I have done my whole life is follow orders and stay in my place and now I have nothing. Well I'm done. I won't lock you up anymore. Do whatever you want, I'm done."

Just like that, Officer left.

Barely able to contain myself, I ran and ran and ran and ran. I have never actually run before, yet my body knew that was exactly what I needed to do. I didn't care if anyone saw me, I didn't care if I fell or got hurt, I just needed to go, somewhere, anywhere.

When I couldn't run anymore, when I couldn't fight it anymore, I found a field full of corn and collapsed.

5

Screaming, all I can hear is screaming and I'm not even sure if it was coming from me. I open my eyes and I see a woman peering over me looking absolutely terrified. People rush over from every direction, dropping whatever work they were doing, children run outside to see what all the commotion is about. In a matter off seconds a huge crowd has gathered and I am the subject of what feels like a thousand pairs of eyes. I wasn't sure what was more intense, the harsh gaze of the people or the bleeding rays of the sun beating me. I felt dizzy. I felt vulnerable. I felt like I was going to be sick. As the crowd continued to stare at me, a man pushed through and slowly walked towards me. I was sitting up at this point, alarmed by such a large amount of attention. The man crouched down just as slowly and pulled off my hat, releasing my plumes of voluminous hair in the process. The people gasped.

"There is evil on our land. This is the manifestation of a curse on our people."

At his proclamation, the women burst out with cries of hysteria. I was shaking, what kind of evil was there?

"I have never seen one, but I have heard about it. This creature is a sign of evil. It appears in human form, but do not be deceived, it is a spirit. It does not eat and drink as we do It cannot see and feel as we can. It has the eyes of a demon, red like hellfire. Its mother is a witch. It carries bad luck wherever it goes."

As the man continued to speak, the crowd became more tense, moving slightly away with every new sentence. I was shocked to hear the things the man was saying about me. How can I be evil? Why would he say these things? He clearly doesn't know what he is talking about, for example I have brown eyes.

The crowd kept oo-ing and ah-ing which urged the man to get louder in his address.

"This creature is a specimen of pure evil, my people. The only way for us to rid ourselves of this pollution is to kill him." At this point, my jaw dropped. My eyes expanded to a size that I didn't know they could reach. I turned and looked at this man in utter disbelief. Were they really going to kill me?

"My people, it is well known that once harvested, the body parts of the creature are extremely lucky, they bring good fortune to whoever possesses them. That is why we must do this tonight. Creature, get up. We must take you to see the witchdoctor."

Before I knew it, I was dragged up and a group of men much stronger than me surrounded me and marched me behind the old man. I could hear the noise of the crowd following behind but I couldn't make myself look back. We all moved together through a forest that was as wild as that in the Wasteland. The further we got into the forest, the more trees I saw with red and white ribbons tied around them, even the sound of the wind whistling through the leaves became grave. There were trails of bones scattered on the ground but I tried not to focus too much on this until I kicked something believing it to be a rock, only to look down and see a skull. The further we got in, the darker the light fell, even the noise of the crowd began to subside. I tried closing my eyes, to try and shake the reality away, but the men just began pushing me along the trail. We carried on like this for sometime, when suddenly, a voice broke through

"Stop. Stop."

A man ran through the crowd and stood in the face of the elder, leading the pack.

"Let me take the boy. I've seen one before, I know what to do. Let me take him"

The elder responded.

"No. The creature must meet its fate with the gods. We will take him to the Witchdoctor. Step away."

"Let me take him, let me be responsible for the pollution. I am new in this zone, let me do this one thing for the people."

I stared at the elder, desperate to see if he would let me go with this new man, not sure if my fate would be better with him but eager to not be the subject of such a spectacle by the crowd.

"Young man, you have noble intentions. I will release the boy to you but everyone here will bear witness to the fact that if any evil does befall this land, if you fail to appease the gods on account of this creature, you will pay the ultimate price."

At his words, the crowd quickly dispersed, too happy to

leave this evil forest, and the elder followed slowly behind them, frequently turning back at us and giving discerning looks.

When the people were no longer in sight, I looked up at the man with total relief and fear in my eyes. He nodded at me and then without saying a word, proceeded to walk in a different direction out of the forest. Unable to do anything else, I followed him and we walked in complete silence. We continued like that, even when we got out of the forest and back to the neat fields and eventually, we came to a building and he let me in. There was no one else there, and from the looks of things, there would be no one else joining us. The main room was small, furnished with one chair and a rug and there was a little stove at the back. There were no pictures or anything else to indicate that another person lived here with him.

"You must be starving, let me heat up some rice for you."

I watched him bring the rice over and gladly received it.

"You're not going to kill me are you?" I asked just as I was about to feed the rice into my mouth.

"No, you're safe. I promise."

I quickly ate my rice. It was evening now and I hadn't eaten since I left the prison. I had forgotten how hungry I was. When all the food was gone, I looked up at the man who was drinking a bottle of beer, leaning against the fridge in the corner.

"Why did you save me?"

"Sorry?"

"Why? Why did you save me? You could have allowed the witchdoctor to kill me."

He put the beer down and I could see a change in him as he began.

"I come from another Two zone. After I was born, my mother fell pregnant again. She had a baby that was like you. As soon as word came out, my mother and the baby were killed. My father's business was boycotted, nobody would help us. We were forced out of the zone and had to resettle somewhere where our story was not known. My father died not long after from sadness and so I became something of a wanderer. I saved your life because I know the truth, it is not people like you that are evil, it is them, the people who think it is okay to kill the innocent that are evil."

I was moved by his story.

"My mother is dead too, that's why I came here, to see her." I told him my story, about Aunty Gloria and Officer, about the prison, I even told him all the things that Officer told me before he left. He stood there and listened to me speak all night and when I was done, he walked over to me, looked me in the eyes and said

"You have to go to Capital. You have to find out who you are and why you were sent here. The fact that you were sent away and that specific plans were made for your life means that you are not just any random albino. One of your parents must be extremely powerful."

"But how can I do that? How can I find out who my parents are? How can I get to Capital?"

"I don't know how you'll do it but you have to try. I can't get in to One and Upper zones but I can definitely smuggle you into a Middle zone. I distribute my vegetables to the Middle zones just south of here. I'm going next the day after tomorrow. I can hide you in the back of my truck behind some crates and when we cross the border, we will figure out a way for you to keep going.

Trust me, it is really important that you do this. For your own sake, you need to know who you are."

I thought about this heavily. Yesterday I had only ever met two people, I had never experienced the outside world, now an adventure had been thrust upon me and I had to decide if I could take it. I remembered all the books I read and all the heroes I had cheered on. I felt like I had become one of them. This felt like one of those moments where the answer had already been decided for me.

"Okay, I'm doing it."

"Good. Now you need to get your rest Kanmi. We have a long journey ahead of us."

The man, Ohi, switched the lights off in the main room and made his way to one of the other rooms. Before he went inside, he said.

"By the way, you probably shouldn't go out of the house without me. The people here think you are dead and if they find out that you're still alive, they will come for the both of us."

I lay on the carpet trying to fall asleep but my mind will not let me. I couldn't come to terms with everything that I had learnt over the last 48 hours. However, what was most distressing was the fact that I was a fugitive. I was a wanted man because of the colour of my skin. At least the prisoners in the Wasteland were given the courtesy of actually committing a crime before they were punished. People looked at me and didn't see a person. They just saw me as some evil creature that should be harvested. This truly sickened me to the point where I felt Goosebumps appear all over my skin. What kind of world did I live in?

I woke up the next morning to the sound of music. Ohi was singing along to Fela Kuti as he was mixing something at the stove. I remember the song because Officer used to love Fela's music. His favourite song was "Beast of No Nation' because he says that even now, the Fathers who rule are still as corrupt as those that used to rule in Fela's time. My back hurt, I had slept badly.

"Porridge?"

Ohi had seen me, he was walking over with a steaming bowl.

"So what are we doing today?" I asked as I took the bowl from him.

"Today we will make a plan. We have to be careful about our adventure. We are working against not only the culture of the land, but also the law of the land. Honey?"

"Yes please. So you've already said that I'll hide with the vegetables. When we cross the border, what next?"

"Here's the honey. Give me time. I will have a plan by the end of the day"

Ohi was gone that whole day. He was busy packing the vegetables for delivery the next day. He told me to clean myself up and gave me clothes to change into. I was relieved to wash all that dirt off my body and wear something that wasn't uniform. I had been dressed in uniform ever since I moved into the prison. As it turns out, my prison worker uniform was unnecessary as my job at the prison was a front. It was weird staring at myself in the mirror. I did have a small mirror in the bathroom at the prison but the room was so dimly lit that I really couldn't see myself in it. I always cut myself shaving and not shaving wasn't an option with Officer constantly on the prowl. I had never seen myself like this before. I felt how defined my cheekbones are, my lips were so full and pink, I had never noticed before. I washed my hair and it was drooping all around my face. I noticed how my hair gleamed when the light hit it. I had never really noticed the way my hair curled. I knew it was curly but I didn't realise how tight the individual curls were. I pulled one of the strands to its maximum length and it went all the way to the bottom of my chest. I realised something there and then, my nose is beautiful, my eyes are beautiful, my lips are beautiful, my skin, my hair, my ears, every bit of me. I put on the clothes that Ohi gave me and something overwhelming came over me, I was proud. I looked good, there was nothing wrong with me and I was going to find out who I really was. I was finally living a life.

"By one of the markets I distribute to, there is a taxi firm. I've often noticed that the drivers head towards the zones of the Uppers and Ones just as I finish unpacking the vegetables. Here is what we are going to do. When we get to the market, I'll pack my truck like I usually do, then we will start a fire with the rubbish there. There is usually a lot of rubbish from the packaging that they throw out but I will pack a bottle of petrol just to make things quick. Once the fire is up and running, I will rush over to the taxi firm and I will ask whichever driver is inside to open the boot of their car to lend me his fire extinguisher. I will then rush him to the scene of the fire, forcing him to neglect closing the boot of the car, at which point, you will go inside the boot and close it shut, but before you enter the boot, you must make a very tiny puncture in one of the front tires of the car so that the driver has a reason for opening the boot later on for you to make your escape. It will be very early in the morning so there won't be anyone around to catch you, and I will rush those who are around to assist me in putting out the fire. When the fire is out, I will then bring the driver's attention to the time and urge him to start heading to work before he is late. When he passes the border, he will then begin to notice that his tyre is getting flat, at which point he will want to change his tyre. Now this is very important, the minute he begins to open the boot, at the very earliest opportunity, you must use whatever instrument you have at your disposable, even if it means carrying a stone with you, you must use it to strike the driver so that he will jump back and give you enough room to run away. Strike him hard enough so that you have a couple of minutes head start and not just to startle him, remember that you have to get out of the boot first before you can start running away. Once you get into Upper and One territory, it will become a lot easier to make your way to the Capital." This was the plan that Ohi presented to me after we had our dinner. I was confident in our plan. Now I just had to wait.

As it turned out, I didn't have to wait very long. Ohi woke me up at about 1:30am, which, as it turns out, is a perfectly reasonable time for Twos to get up. I quickly shook off all my sleepiness and followed him outside. He led me to the back of his truck which he had already started loading up and then beckoned me to enter it. He had stacked the crates against the three sides of the truck so that I could fit perfectly in the centre of the shape, closer to the front of the truck so he could communicate with me. Once I was slotted in, he continued filling the truck up, even stacking some longer boxes in such a way as to give the appearance of them being stacked on top of me. When the truck had been filled and he was satisfied with his stacking, he locked the back doors of the truck and entered the driver's seat. As soon as I felt the truck begin to jerk forwards, I shut my eyes and closed them tight, this was really happening.

We drove in total silence. I was too nervous to say anything even though I had a thousand questions running through my mind. I couldn't see anything either, it was completely pitch-black and my body was beginning to cramp up. All I could do was focus on the sounds of the vegetables rolling around in their boxes as the truck drove along. Some time later, I felt the truck begin to slow down and then stop altogether.

"Good morning officers, here are my papers."

I tried my best to listen to what the officers were saying but all I could make out from their tone of voice was their hostility. Next thing I knew, I could hear two sets of footsteps approaching Ohi's side of the truck.

"Come down"

Ohi must have complied because I heard him get out of the truck without saying a word. The two footsteps then led Ohi to the back of the truck.

"Open it."

No words can describe the terror I felt in that instant. I was petrified. I couldn't believe it. Again, Ohi complied without making any protest and the double doors of the truck were flung open. Suddenly the darkness was pierced with this blinding shot of light. One of the officers was using a torch to inspect the cargo. The light was burning my eyes but I didn't dare flinch. At a point, he shone the torch directly at me and paused, I could just about see him through the holes in the crate, I could see the harshness in his face. I had been caught. At that moment, Ohi cleared his throat and said

"So you see officers, I have nothing to hide. Nothing here is out of the ordinary. So can I be on my way now?"

Just like that, the officers closed the doors and grumbled back into their stations. Ohi got back into the truck and we were off. I could barely contain myself, my heart was beating outside of my chest, my hands were shaking in disbelief. The plan was taking shape.

I really wanted to see what the Middle zones looked like. Whenever Ohi would stop the truck to make a delivery, I would try my best to have a quick look around but I could only really see the back of the shops he was delivering to. After I accepted the fact that this was all I was going to see for myself, I decided to ask him "What are Middle zones like?" He said that the Middles weren't farming people like the Twos are so their land is much smaller. Most of them work in the senior zones because they earn more money there. Those who cant get work in the senior regions or prefer not to, start their own businesses if they can and it is very common for the children to be educated through apprenticeships at these small businesses. He said from his experience, the middles were a very stressed people because they lived at the mercy of the senior demes. In fact, it was common knowledge that the senior demes preyed upon the Middles. Every now and again, a story would emerge of a Senior abusing or abducting a Middle for his or her own sadistic reasons, Ohi said that this meant that there must be hundreds of cases which happen that no one knows about. Ohi said that he would much rather be a Two than a middle because at least he got to keep his dignity.

"Okay, we are now driving into the zone that I told you about. Do you remember the plan?" I did remember; start fire, puncture tire, get in the boot, strike the driver and run. "There is a crowbar in the seat next to me, make sure you take it with you." We pulled up to the grocery store; it was still dark outside which made it easy for Ohi to gather up the discarded cardboard boxes and wooden crates without being seen. Once he had a pile large enough, he let me out of the truck and laughed at me for a while, as I was trying to regain feeling in my legs. It wasn't so difficult to get out of the truck because at this point, most of the deliveries had been made. As soon as I was able, I went to retrieve the crowbar and petrol from the passenger's seat. "Will someone not see us?" I asked him as I handed the petrol over. "The woman who runs the shop started the business because she was too old to commute to the senior zones. The people who help her run the shop don't get to work until 6:30. I usually just drop the vegetables inside myself, most of the time I don't even see anyone. We are fine." He doused the pile with a little petrol and then got a lighter and a folded piece of paper from his pocket, lit the paper and dropped it on the pile. Immediately, the fire spread through the pile and I was mesmerized. There was something about the flames, the way they licked the air, desperate for oxygen. The colours too, watching the cold blue dance with the red excited me. But I remembered myself when Ohi grabbed me by the arm and rushed me away from the back of the shop. We hurried down the street just a few buildings down and when we arrived at the taxi office, he told me to crouch against the side of the building, which I did. From there I had a clear view of the place that the taxis were parked. Ohi then ran inside the office and I can only assume that our plan was working well because moments later, the two men had run back to the shop and the car boot really had been left open. I looked around and it was still relatively dark outside, there was no one around. I slowly crept up to the car with the boot open, making sure to move on the side that was covered by the car, then I brought out the nail which Ohi had placed in my breast pocket and pushed it into the tyre by the driver's seat. Once it was firmly in and I felt some air begin to escape, I made my way to the boot. It wasn't until I climbed inside that I realised that there would not be enough space for me to fit in the boot with the spare tyre so I quickly carried the tyre out and dropped it by the wall I was leaning on before rushing back into the boot. Closing it from the inside turned out to be more of a challenge than I anticipated. I saw a hook that I could use to pull the roof down but I didn't manage to jam it shut properly. While I was still struggling with the hook, I heard Ohi's voice and I knew that time was up.

"Yes I know, that was so strange. It was a good thing that I saw it on time otherwise who knows what would have happened. Anyway I better let you get on with your day." I then felt two hard knocks on the boot, which were enough to securely shut it, and by then, I guess Ohi left because I no longer heard his voice. Next thing I know, the ignition of the taxi was started and the car began to drive away. In that moment, I realised how vulnerable I was. I had left the only home that I ever knew and I had lost the only friend that I ever had. Now I was at the mercy of the world and fate, I guess, and the only possession that I had was the crowbar that I clutched so tightly in that dark boot.

Not that long into our drive, I felt the car stop, we were at the border. I felt a little anxious due to my previous experience at the border with Ohi, but this time it went by seamlessly, the car was moving again in minutes. I'm not sure how long we were driving for, I was now used to travelling without being able to see what was going on, I was just enjoying feeling the gentle motion of the car, which was why it was easy for me to notice when the car started to slow down and eventually come to a stop. I felt the car shake a little when the driver stepped out and I wondered if he had finally noticed the flat tyre or if we had reached wherever he was going. Either way, I was ready. I gripped the crowbar as tight as I could and positioned myself to strike. As you would have it, the driver had noticed the tyre and had come round to the back of the car to get the spare. I heard the boot click open, I saw the light rush in, I knew the plan, I knew what I had to do, I was ready. I froze. He continued to open the boot. The more he opened it, the more I was fighting myself to hit him but for whatever reason, I couldn't bring myself to do it.

"Wait, what the hell is going on?"

It was too late now, he had seen me. I had missed my opportunity.

"Who the hell are you?"

I messed up.

6

I was sitting in the passenger seat of the car. Now that I had the opportunity to look at what this zone was like, I didn't want to. I was so disappointed in myself, all I could do was look down and stare at my hands. I really blew it. What was I going to do? The driver was so angry that he refused to enter the car with me. He just stood behind the car, leaning against the boot with his hands crossed until a downpour of rain came and forced him into the car reluctantly. Even when he came in, I didn't look up. I was so ashamed.

"You have cost me my whole day of work. Do you know what that means? There are people who rely on me on a daily basis; I barely make enough to keep us afloat. I don't know what even possessed you to enter my car. What were you trying to do? What did you think would happen? Now we are stuck here in this car, waiting for another driver to bring his spare tyre, but he wont get here for a while, he has to drop off a client first. But better know that the minute he gets here, I am driving back to my Middle zone and straight to the authorities. What they do to you, I don't know, I don't care."

I was somewhat relieved that the man was turned with his back facing me as he angrily smoked his cigarettes out of the rolled down window. I had never seen someone smoke so many cigarettes so quickly but if it meant that he wouldn't look at me, I was happy. I was in such despair, all my planning and my efforts and all the risks that I had taken, everything, wasted because of my weakness. Why can I not hurt others as easily and as readily as others are prepared to hurt me? Why must I be so different to the world around me? I continued to think all these thoughts as we sat in silence in the car. After a while, I noticed something, the driver had fallen asleep. He rested his head against the car door and sat with his hands crossed. Almost as soon as I realised, he began to snore. Then I suddenly had a thought, why was this man so comfortable in my presence? I thought people were supposed to be afraid of me. I thought people hated me. I thought people wanted to kill me. Was I not evil in their eyes? Was I not a devil or did this man not know? Maybe he was like Ohi and had known someone like me. When I think about it, he was angry with me because of what I had done and not because of who I was. I mean, I know I haven't had that many human interactions but this touched me. It was nice to know that I wasn't condemned in the eyes of everyone or that some did not always practice that traditional belief. Perhaps the higher up you are in society, the more likely you are to think more critically and the more open you are to change; both socially and personally. I began to have hope of a life for me in the Upper zones. Maybe they would embrace someone like me since they all are so educated. But just as I was getting deeper into this dream of having a normal life, I remembered what Officer had said, it had been the Uppers, in fact it had been from the very Capital that the order to banish me had come from. There was no hope for me anywhere on this continent. There was no hope for me anywhere in this world. For the first time ever, the truth of this statement really hit me and I began to weep. In fact, I began to mourn myself, and it was ugly. It felt like blood was coming out of my eyes, I could feel the snot seep out of my nose, I couldn't contain the pain in my chest and it came out as a despairing groan from my throat. At this point, I could feel that the man had woken up and was staring at me. His mouth was open and he was shocked I suppose. He obviously was wondering who this lunatic was who had broken in to his car and was now crying so bitterly as he asked "Who are you?"

" I am nobody. I was born and I don't even know my own mother. For whatever reason, the Capital banished me as a baby to live and die in the Wasteland. I have lost the only home I have ever known. The reason I am in your car is because I was trying to get into the capital to try and find out why they condemned me to such a life of sadness. I'm trying to see if I can learn something about my mother or my father, so I can understand who I am. I need to know where I fit in because so far, the only consistent thing in my life is the fact that I don't fit in. I've lived my whole life on this continent. I eat the food, I speak the language, I wear the same clothes, I have the same hair, yet, everywhere I go, I am seen as an outcast. I need to know who my parents are, where I come from because even if I don't fit in anywhere, I must fit in there."

"Young man, let me tell you something, you don't want to fit in this place. The society we live in was deliberately designed to supress any form of individuality. It is a disgusting society and perhaps what is most disgusting of all is that fact that many people have given up on finding themselves and have chosen to live their lives in the grey of mob mentality. You think I don't know what people think about children like you? I know. But if I am totally honest, I am jealous of you. Whether you like it or not, you have to stand out of the crowd, you have to be your own person. That is not to say that you cannot associate with them or live like them because you are just as much of a member of this land as the next man, but you have a higher calling, one which is as obvious as daylight, one which you cannot run or hide from. "

After he said this, he paused and pulled out his wallet from his back pocket. From within the wallet, he brought out two folded up photographs. He opened up the smaller one and handed it to me.

"I hate this system so much, I have lost too much to it. When I was younger my father was taken away from me, and then my sister. When my sister, who was about 16 at the time, didn't come back, my mother almost died of grief. But she had to be strong for me. I was all that she had left. I wish I could be like you so I could break away from this system. I have spent many nights thinking about what I would say to that wicked man Abisogun, but that is only talk. Someone like me can never actually meet him let alone confront him. Plus I have a family to consider." He unfolds the second picture and hands it to me. "If I ever stepped out of line and got myself arrested, what would happen to them? I just have to accept my fate."

I stared intensely at the second picture he had given me.

"Tell me about your family." I asked.

My wife is Ife. We have been together now for 10 years. She runs a little bakery outside our house, it doesn't earn much but I insisted that she didn't work outside of our zone. We have a daughter, Morenike, the love of my life, she's only seven but she looks so much like her mother, everyone says she has my eyes though. Every now and again, I see a bit of my sister in her, she is incredibly caring and quite mature for her age. The other picture in your hand is my sister, Funke. That was taken the year before my father left, when we were still very happy."

"What happened to her?"

"Good question, I don't know, I wish I could say. One day she left to find work in the higher zones and I never heard from her again. I knew something was wrong because she didn't even tell me she was going, talk-less of saying goodbye. I remember how hurt I was the night she left. I couldn't believe she just left me. When my mother came back home to visit me, I asked her if she had heard from Funke and she was totally taken aback, she didn't even know that Funke had left. It was from then on that she resigned from her work in the higher zones and began living with me again. I however decided to become a taxi driver like my father was, in the hope that one day, I might run into my sister and bring her back home or at least, get in touch with her. But as the years have gone by, it feels less likely that I will find her. I know what happens to young girls who come to look for work here. Many of them end up becoming prostitutes, even if they didn't set out to be. The ones who do find work as house-helps or waitresses or whatever tend to get abused by the men around them. The way these higher demes treat us is despicable. To them, we are the scum beneath their shoes, we are there for their own pleasure. It's terrible because we are trapped, we don't have a choice but to go and work for them but in working for them, we are putting ourselves in danger. I mean, how can a man put his own 16 year old daughter in school and chase away boys her age from talking to her, yet he is beating up another 16 year old girl and forcing himself on her every night just because he is paying her salary? It's wickedness. Yet we can't escape the reality of the situation; if you don't work, you die, if you do work, you die. I personally like to think that Funke is a schoolteacher somewhere or a chef in a hotel or something. Maybe even with a fiancé if not married, she could even be living in another Middle zone, which is still a possibility. I don't really care what she is doing, as long as she is safe. But there has been no sign of her for the past 23 years, I don't know, its all in God's hands."

It was evident how much the man loved his sister, it was evident how much his family meant to him. It was funny, as we sat in the car and exchanged stories of our lives and our misfortunes, I felt like we shared a bond. It was this strange feeling of a meeting that was fated to happen, like my plan had to fail and we had to have this exact conversation. For whatever reason, I felt like we needed to speak to one another and it was nice, it renewed my conviction in what I was doing. We continued to talk like this, so candidly, so openly about our lives until the person who was bringing the tyre came and the tyre was fitted on.

He got back in the car and shut the door. Without saying a word he just put the key in the ignition, turned the car around and headed back towards his zone. I was a little surprised by this, after all of our conversations I was under the impression that he was supporting my mission. I thought that it was safe to assume that he was not going to hand me over to the authorities anymore.

"Where are we going?" I asked

"Home."

It was very late when we got to his house, or at least it seemed late, I had to get back into the boot of the car to cross the border again. Once we were in the house I immediately felt a warmth so strong that it penetrated even the deepest chambers of my heart. The pungent odour of fresh bread was such a luxury, I was already anticipating dinner, even if it would be just the bread. I was happy. I noticed that his wife liked having soft furnishings around the house, just like Aunty Gloria, and that made me smile. As soon as the man walked through the door, his daughter Morenike ran over and gave her daddy a hug and he in return gave her a kiss on the forehead, which was really touching, officer did not like me hugging him when I was younger so I learnt very early not to.Similarly, his wife Ife came over to him and gave him a kiss to welcome him back.

"You are welcome into our little home." she said to me after noticing me shyly standing behind him.

"Thank you."

"Come Kanmi, let me introduce you to my mother."

He led me further into the house. It was a small house, the main room acted as the living room and dining room, beside the main room, there was a small kitchen the size of a hallway which, in all honesty, was the only room I was interested in. There were two doors on the opposite side of the kitchen, both bedrooms

I assume as the man and I had already gone to use the public bathrooms before we came into the house. We got to one of the bedrooms and knocked on the door softly.

"Come in." said the voice of the elderly woman on the inside and at her beckoning, the man opened the door. We didn't actually go into the room however, there was not enough space, the room was only big enough to house a bed, a wardrobe and a beside table which were already pushing against each other so we just stood by the door. From there it was very difficult to actually see the woman herself, mainly because the room was lit by a solitary candle placed on her bedside table, but I did make out the bible that lay on the table beside it, just like Aunty Gloria used to have.

"Mummy, this is Adekanmi. He is our guest for tonight."

"Good evening ma" I said, trying to look at her as sincerely as I could. At this, I could see her vague figure get up from the bed and begin to walk towards me but the closer she got to me, the more I could tell that something was wrong. She was wearing a long kaftan which caught the wind and made her slow movements seem even more dramatic, she seemed to float eerily towards me with both her hands placed on her head, I couldn't help but look at her hair, although it was a low-cut style, the strength of the silvery colour shone through and it made me wonder if it had greyed earlier in her life from all the tragedies that the man had told me about their life. She stood directly in front of me and I could see that even with the warmth of the candle reflecting in her eyes, there was still an overwhelming coldness there. Even the taxi driver could see the alarm in the old woman. He rushed over to her and held her arms in a supportive embrace.

"Mummy what is it?"

"Folusho, who is this?" she whispered in a barely-there voice. Although the question was directed at the driver, she didn't once take her eyes away from me.

"He is Adekamni, I told you. I just met him today, what is it mummy?"

"Folusho can you not see? Look at him, can you not see?"

The driver slowly lifted his head from his mother and turned his gaze to me. He began breathing heavily now and I could see the same alarm glaze over his eyes too. At this point I didn't know which of them I ought to be looking at. They were scaring me and I didn't even know why. The old woman broke the silence and asked me,

"Adekanmi, who is your mother?"

"I don't know ma. I don't know my birth mother."

"Folusho, how long has your sister been missing now?"

"23 years mummy."

"Adekanmi, how old are you?"

"Almost 22 ma." At this point, I could feel myself trembling. What was going on?

The old woman reached for my hand with both her hands and held on to it.

"Adekanmi, your face, your eyes, you look exactly like my daughter, exactly like Funke."

My throat became dry, my heart felt like it had stopped.

"Huh?"

Folusho pulled out his wallet faster than I could shut my eyes and within seconds, that same picture that I had been looking at in the car was in my hands. They were right. I did look like her. Could she be my mother?

7

The night that followed was so awkward. Folusho and his mother could not keep their eyes off me and the more I caught them staring at me, the more irritated I became because I could feel them giving me this hope with every glance, and for something so important, so monumental, something literally life changing, I didn't want them to be wrong. Folusho made a plan. A friend of his, Ikenna, was a nurse at one of the hospitals in a One zone. Like most other Middles, he had learnt his trade through apprenticeship from a young age. Ikenna was to come and take blood samples of me and Folusho's mother and then sneak the samples into the hospital under anonymous names to be tested. Sure enough, Ikenna came the next night and collected our blood. He also didn't seem too concerned about my colour, or if he was, he didn't show it. All he said was that he owed Folusho a favour and that we would hear back in the next couple of days. Every night felt like hell. Both for

Folusho's mother and I. She locked herself in her room and did nothing but scream prayers and shout songs to God, hoping that this was her miracle. I on the other hand was a lot less vocal about my anxiety. The truth of the matter was that ever since I left the Wasteland, my life had taken off at such an exceptional speed that I was feeling lost somewhere. After years of literally being trapped, now everything was opening up to me, I might even have a real family of my own. I spent those days just playing with Morenike, she was always very happy to sit and talk to me, especially when her mother was downstairs at the bakery. It was nice, I had never had a sibling or a friend for that matter so having her around was really heart-warming. I guess what touched me the most was how open she was to me, she wanted to introduce me to her friends and to the people who shop at the bakery and got upset when I told her that this wasn't a very good idea. She wasn't afraid to touch me or to be near me, she called me her friend. I know that she is a child but its just interesting to think that of all of the people who hated me enough to kill me in that Two zone, all of the children there would have been as receptive as she is, the only difference being that they grew up in households that painted me as being this monster. The whole system is just very sad.

The days went on and each day seemed to get longer than the next, but surely enough, one night Folusho came home with the news. He just walked in the door, walked over to me and gave me this tight hug. As he was hugging me, he started to cry and this was when I knew. The hug lasted for what seemed like a long time and when he finally composed himself, we went together to tell his mother. She too burst out in tears and he went to hug her this time. I was in shock, I didn't know what to do. Now I knew who my mother was but I still had not met her and from what Folusho had said, I probably never would meet her. However I didn't want to think about that now, I just wanted to enjoy the moment. I had found a piece of my puzzle. As I was thinking these things leaning against the door of Folusho's mother's room, Folusho beckoned me to come and sit next to the both of them on the bed.I walked over and sat by my grandmother and she held my hand again and said to me

"You are home now."

8

I stayed with Folusho for some time, partly because now that I knew I belonged there, I had this peace of mind that I had never experienced ever in my life, and partly also because my grandmother would not let me as much as step out of the house. In the time that I stayed, life was good. I was happy. Everyday seemed better than the last. I was making memories with my family and it was more than I ever thought I would get from this adventure. On my 22st birthday, Ife had surprised me and cooked my favourite meal, plantain and jollof rice, and baked this beautiful chocolate cake. My grandmother had even gone out of her way to make me buba and sokoto from the most decadent blue fabric, I was even surprised that they knew because the only person I had told about my birthday was Morenike, only because she had asked me when I had just come to the home. Folusho took me to the local bar to celebrate and this was a huge moment for me because it was the first time that I went to a public place in this zone, I knew that my family were open and accepting of me but I wasn't sure how others would react to me. I didn't voice my concern to Folusho but I know he must have felt it, he kept on patting my shoulders almost as a way to reinforce the fact that everything would be ok. It was interesting, as soon as we entered the bar, I could feel every single pair of eyes in the place on me, now as someone who is naturally shy anyway, this was excruciating. I had never seen the attention of so many men be diverted from a football match. We made our way slowly to the bar because every few feet, some grizzly man would come and greet Folusho in an equally grizzly manner, their approach to me on the other hand was less overtly direct, some would stare at me while others would try their best not to.

"Folusho, what can I start you off with tonight?" said the bartender, wiping a glass cup as he spoke.

"You know my usual Lekan. Orijin, cold one."

"And for the oyinbo?" I assumed he was asking about me.

"He will have one too. Cold."

For the rest of the night, that was how people referred to me, oyinbo pepe. I asked Folusho what it meant as I had never heard it before and he said that it was an affectionate way to address people who had very fair skin. I didn't like it. As the men became more and more drunk, a chorus formed and they even sang me a song, some sort of nursery rhyme about this mystical 'oyinbo pepe'. I still didn't like it, but I smiled sheepishly, at least they weren't trying to kill me. It's interesting, in the worst of times, my difference could be the cause of my death and in the best of times, the cause of my ridicule. Despite all of this, I did have a really good night. I realised for the first time the power of alcohol. I sang football songs with my arms draped around strange men, I was made something of a celebrity and it was fun. I think Folusho spent most of the night laughing at me to be honest. We went home happy.

Folusho sat me down one day when the house was completely empty, a couple of weeks after that night, and we had a very serious conversation.

"Kanmi, do you remember when we first met, you were on your way to the Capital. You were going to challenge the Fathers to find out why they had sent you to the Wasteland. Do you remember?"

"Yes, I do. Why?"

"I've been thinking about this for sometime now and I really don't want you to lose focus. I think that it is important that you do this. Primarily for your sake, but also for our sake too."

"What do you mean?"

"You see, ever since I found out that Funke is your mother, I realised that the Fathers must have something to do with her disappearance also, maybe just like they tried to make you disappear. I think that it is time for you to further your journey and find out what happened."

I was a little thrown off by this, I hadn't considered leaving for a long time, I was enjoying being a part of my family too much. But I understood what Folusho was saying, it was important that I completed what I started, even more so.

"So when should I leave? How will I get there?"

"Leave at the end of next week, so that you have enough time to prepare. Based on what you said before, you didn't have much of a plan when you tried to get to the Capital before but this time, you have to really be prepared. You can't sneak around and try and hide when you get to the Upper and One zones, the security there is much tighter, if they see you, they will kill you on the spot. We have to find a way for you to get there in the open."

"In the open? How?"

"Okay I have it. I have seen people like you in the Ones before, well not people like you per se, foreign people with yellow skin and yellow hair. If we make you look less African and more foreign, change your name, we could get away with it."

"So what should I be called?"

"George Peterson, a European expatriate who grew up overseas. You are visiting Africa for leisure purposes."

"Ok. George Peterson. Start calling me this now so I get used to it."

"Alright…George."

Over that week I went through a lot of transformations, Grandmother and Folusho went out to try and source the most European looking clothes they could, including a suit which I had never seen in real life. However, the biggest transformation of them all must have been my hair. Ife sat me down and not only did she cut my hair much shorter than it had ever been cut, she also permed it with chemical relaxer in order to make it straight and bouncy like the white people on TV and on billboards. I didn't like it at all but as she said,

"Its hair, it'll grow back."

Folusho also tried to teach me European mannerisms and an accent but I think that all his efforts were in vain because, even though I don't know how the Europeans talk, I'm pretty sure it wasn't what he was doing.

After several hours of learning how to walk, talk, eat, dress and act like a European, I was finally ready to leave my family and journey to the Capital. After a heartfelt goodbye, especially to grandmother, I headed out of the zone, once again concealed in Folusho's boot.

Once we were safely over the border and well into a One zone, Folusho let me out of the boot and we continued to drive. We got much further into the zone than we did the other time and I had my first real experience of wealth. Skyscrapers, flashing lights, dual carriage roads, beautiful monuments, water fountains, parks, the whole place was a complete contrast to everything I had ever seen. I couldn't believe that people lived like this, what was even worse was the fact that majority of these people would have no idea how people like us lived just beyond these borders. Eventually we came to the border of the Upper zone. Folusho winded down his window and handed the guard his papers as he would do ordinarily. I on the other hand was less composed. The guard came out and tapped on my window with his baton.

"And you?" he said, not even bothering to look at me

"He is-" began Folusha

"Shut up, who is talking to you?"

I wound down my window and, in the best half Europeanised casual accent I could, said

"George Peterson, I am visiting Africa for a few weeks from Belgium. I'm sorry, I don't have my papers on me right now, I hope this will not be a problem."

My heart was pounding against my chest cavity but I gave the officer the smoothest smile I could muster up. All I could think about was "Shaken, not stirred" I didn't even know what it meant but Folusho said that that was the secret to being European.

As soon as the guard saw this, the most enormous grin covered his face and he was shining his yellowed teeth at me.

"Ah, no problem sir. Its okay, you can go. Oya, Waheed, open the barrier, they are from abroad o."

And just like that, we were free to go. I suddenly understood what Folusho was saying. The only way for me to reach the capital was to capitalise on this insatiable desire to be hospitable and accommodating of foreigners, even to the point of absurdity.

The Upper zone was not as I had imagined it. It was more residential than the One zone, it also seemed like there was substantially fewer people residing there. All the buildings here were painted white with matching picket fences bordering the perfect garden on each lawn. I found the fences so funny because they obviously had no functional properties, as Folusho had told me before, the heavy security presence could definitely be felt as there were armed guards stationed every few blocks and even some patrolling the streets. Its worth noting here that unlike the other divisions, the Uppers really only had one zone and I guess this is due to the fact that the Uppers, again, unlike all other demes, have the luxury of having very extravagant social lives. An integral part of being an Upper is networking and this often meant attending and throwing the most lavish events. This is because status is everything to an Upper and marriage and business is more or less currency, with one often leading to the other. Despite all the opulence that comes with being an Upper, it is perhaps a more savage and ruthless deme because unlike the

Ones who just have money, the Uppers also have the weight of their family name and legacy to fight for and maintain and so they are a lot more cut-throat and two-faced to each other. Right in the centre of the Upper zone is the Capital, and based on everything I've heard, only a select few Uppers have access to it, so finding my way in will not be easy.

Folusho parked the car in front of a glass building. It was extremely tall, about 20 floors or so, and it was designed in the shape of a spiral. It reminded me of those cheap wax candles Aunty Gloria used to put on cakes she would make for my birthday.

"Look, Adekanmi, I can't take you any further than this. If you are going to get into the Capital, you need to start thinking on your feet, but even more important than that, you need to be confident, ridiculously so. These people are all entitled, they can smell weakness, so you need to find some and win them over. You need to be charming. If you play this 'foreign' charade well, this will be your greatest asset. You won't even need to spend a lot of money."

He reached to get my bag, which was on the back seats and placed it on my lap. Then he retrieved a large brown envelope from the glove compartment and handed it to me.

"Put this in your bag, it's a phone and some cash, it's not a lot but it's all I have. Call me anytime, I've already put my number in there. Also, before you go, take this photo of your mother so that you have a constant reminder of why you are doing this" it was the same one he had shown me in his wallet "God be with you."

Just like that, he drove away and I was all alone again, with no idea of what to do. As I was walking towards the hotel doors, I noticed that there were a lot of expensive cars parked, cars that

I had only seen on TV, the sort of cars that the men in the bar that Folusho had taken me to dreamed of getting inside, talk-less of owning. The place was incredibly busy. As soon as I walked through those doors, the first thing I could feel was the blast of the air conditioning, I had never experienced such breeze in all my life, I was used to heat sticking to me like the perpetual sweat on my forehead. A woman wearing a kente dress with a name tag reading "Vanessa" walked up to me. I assumed she worked there because I could see other women wearing the same dress dashing around the lobby, all looking busy with a smile on their faces.

"Good afternoon sir, you must be here for the reception. Let me escort you to the great hall at the back. We can keep your luggage for you if you would like."

As she was speaking, before I had the chance to reply, a man wearing trousers and a hat from the same kente fabric took my bag from me and disappeared with it. I just nodded my head slyly to her and she proceeded to lead me to the hall. I couldn't believe how easy that was.

The hall was unlike anything I had ever seen. There was an aisle down the middle of the room with lots of tables and chairs decadently laid out on both sides. There were flower decorations almost touching the low hanging diamond chandeliers, there were ice sculptures standing at every corner of the room, there were waiters carrying trays of food that never seemed to run out. The room was flooded with blue and purple lights and the place was full of a multitude of people all in the middle of private conversations, all looking as if they could be the ones hosting the event.

"Bride or groom?" she asked me

"'Groom" I answered rather impulsively.

She led me to a table on the left side of the room and then once I sat down, she ushered a waiter to pour me a drink and then went away. I took my drink and continued to survey the room as I drank it. There were about 7 other people sat on my table and it was as though none of them had noticed me sit down amongst them. There were many men sat on this side of the room, most of which were by far older than me, half of which were talking to other men their age, the other half were talking to young women probably my age. I didn't really know how to blend in with this crowd. Everyone was dressed in aso ebi, but here I was wearing a white shirt and chino trousers. It was formal enough I guess.

"So how long are you in Africa for?" said one of the many old men in the gathering.

"I'm here for two more weeks, visiting from Belgium." I didn't even know what I was saying.

"Ah, Alhaji Abdulfatai Usman. Oil and Gas" he stretched out his hand to shake mine. I reciprocated.

"George Peterson. Banker."

"Ah, banking? What sector? You seem to me as an investment banker, no?"

"Yes, actually I am. But I'm still learning the ropes."

"Ok, ok. Which firm?"

"Well I'm currently trying to get my foot in the door but I would like to work for Goldman Sachs or JP Morgan one day"

"Very good my boy, you have ambition."

"Thank you."

"So how do you know Timileyin?" I froze, I didn't know what to say.

"I don't actually know him" I blushed "I'm staying at this hotel and I sort of wondered in, I'm sorry." He laughed.

"Its ok. This is Africa, half these people don't know who the bride and groom are. So who do you know in Africa? Who has been showing you around?"

"I don't actually know anyone here, I've just been travelling around the different demes. I only recently just came to this Upper deme. I find it fascinating how the continent is organised. "

"Ah, interesting, what did you study at school? Political science?"

"Yes, I did. You're good at guessing these things."

"So did I. I have a good mind" he laughs again "Well why don't you save yourself some money and come and be my guest? I have plenty of rooms to spare. Plus you can ask me anything you want about our social structures, it is a topic I very much like to discuss. Plus, my wife Halima is extremely hospitable, we would be honoured to have you as our guest."

"That is a very kind offer, I would hate to impose though."

"Nonsense my boy, ask anyone here, I don't ever say something unless I mean it. Come George."

"In that case, it would be my utmost pleasure to stay with you, thank you."

"Good. Okay let me introduce you to some of my friends here. This is Senator Akinbode, he and I have been doing business together since we were fresh out of school. Senator, this is George Peterson, an investment banker from Belgium, he will be staying with me while he is here." I shook the senator's hand.

"Its nice to meet you" I said

"Hmm" replied the senator, leering at me over his spectacles.

He seemed to be a man of little words, preferring to speak with his eyebrows than with actual words. Alhaji introduced me to another of his friends, Chief Nnamdi Eze. He was a lot more conversable, and a lot less frightening, probably due to the fact that he was the youngest of the three. The four of us talked about a lot of things at that table, or rather, the three of them spoke and I nodded vigorously. The topics ranged from the customary chat about business and politics to surveying the bridesmaids and then competitively bragging about their sons, the latter conversations heavily influenced by the scotch they were drinking I presume.

As we were talking, I noticed two men enter the room. They were obviously very big deals because as they made their way down the carpet in the middle of the aisle, they were proceeded by a band of talking drum players singing salutations to them and spraying money on them. The chief caught me staring and said

"George, do you know who they are? That is Taiwo Famiyesin and Jonathan Dodou, they are two of the five Fathers of our continent. Famiyesin is the Father for the Ones and Dodou is the Father for the Middles." Alhaji interjected

"Yes, I don't know how much you know about our continent but it is the Fathers who rule us. The idea for this kind of Presbyterian leadership stems from our cultural heritage and great reverence for our elders and forefathers. Respect for ones ancestors is imperative to us Africans, therefore it was only natural that when the PanAfrican reform happened, we disregarded democracy and decided to turn to our history. "

"Yes" I said, "I have heard about your system. But does it work?"

Alhaji replied with a smirk "It works for us anyway."

"I see. " I said, disgusted by his answer. But why should I be disgusted, I knew this was the truth anyway.

"In fact my eldest daughter Onyinye is engaged to the son of the Father of All. " boasted the chief, bursting with contentment. "The traditional wedding is taking place in two months. Look at her, somewhere over there, she is the one wearing pink dancing on the stage, she will make such a wonderful wife. As soon as the wedding takes place, when our families are officially joined together, my business will triple and I will finally be awarded this contract to extract oil from one of the Two zones that I have been hoping on for years. But best of all, when she has a son, he will also become an elder and my bloodline will have real political power."

Alhaji teased him "We know ah, Nnamdi you will not kill us with this your news. Don't worry, we will come and be merry and drink palm wine on the day too. But don't forget us when your time of enjoyment comes o."

"Ah, never, my friend. You too must share out of my fortune."

The men laughed and I choked out a laugh too for the sake of blending in. So this was how things worked for the rich. Okay.

We continued to drink and talk until the men decided that it was time to go, even though the party had no sign of being over. Alhaji asked me if I wanted to come home with him now or if I would prefer to stay and party with the young people. I decided to stay, to which he arranged to go home with the Senator, leaving his driver outside to bring me home when I was ready. I thanked him and said goodbye to all the men, before then making my way to the front of the room where I could see a whole host of people dancing and drinking. It was interesting to think that these people were all around my age yet they were everything I wasn't; all highly educated in their shiny clothes, perfect hair and teeth, excellently versed, they were just better. I decided to go and mingle with the men who were standing by the door that led to the veranda, mainly smoking cigars and drinking. They were all dressed in perfectly fitted suits that cost more than the income of every Two and Middle family combined, and they were all so well groomed, with thick beards that looked like they could have been carved from marble, causing me to question my own masculinity. One guy saw me walking over and introduced himself to me.

"Hey man, I'm Uti. Whats your name?"

"George."

"George, do you smoke?" I didn't.

"Yeah, sure, okay." He handed me a fresh cigar and lit it. I took one puff and almost died. The guys were in hysterics and I would have been embarrassed if I wasn't still wheezing for air.

"Don't worry, we were all like that" said, another guy, Mathew.

I guess my little episode broke the ice because the other guys were more receptive of me after that. I explained to them how I was visiting from Belgium and a couple of the guys in the group said that they had visited Belgium a couple of times while they where at university, luckily they didn't actually ask me anything that would catch me out. As we were talking, I noticed two girls, one of whom had been one of the bridesmaids the men had been talking about previously, come over to us. They were both beautiful. The bridesmaid smiled a smile so radiant that it caused the throng of men to disperse right in front of her and she stopped right in front of myself and Uti.

"Uti, what time do you want to go home? I'm getting pretty tired and I have to be at the hospital tomorrow morning. "

"I think I'm going to go out with the boys from here actually, let me get someone to drop you home. Oh, by the way, Chi, this is my friend George, he is around for a couple of weeks. George, this is my little sister Chioma."

"Nice to meet you" I said, and I really meant it. She was beautiful.

The truth of the matter was that I never really had the opportunity to meet any girls at all and all of a sudden, here I was, in a room with undoubtedly the most beautiful girls in Africa.

"Actually, Uti, I have a car waiting for me outside. I can drop you home Chioma if you don't mind directing the driver." I was a little hesitant after I said this, I wasn't sure if she'd actually take me up on my offer. I instantly felt foolish.

"That's really kind of you George. Yeah, that would be great. But is it okay if my friend Lulu came with us? She is staying at mine tonight. "

"Of course, I don't see why that should be a problem." Uti tapped me on the back

"Thanks George, I really appreciate it. Some of the boys and I are actually going out for lunch tomorrow, you should come, 3pm give or take half an hour at the Pavilion, we will be sat at the waterfront, is that cool?"

"Yes, I'll see you then. Thanks for the cigar" They laughed.

Chioma, Lulu and I made our way outside as soon as I had retrieved my bag from the concierge. As soon as I stepped out, a man approached me. He looked a little older than me, possibly in his thirties. I assumed that he was Alhaji's driver because he was wearing a uniform. I was surprised that he knew who I was instantly and when I asked him, he said

"Ah ah, oga told me to look out for the oyinbo man."

Oh. That word again.

The girls and I waited for the driver to bring out the car and when he pulled up, I was in awe. It was a G-wagon jeep, black and matte. I wouldn't even have been able make it out if the headlights were not on. It looked like a shadow, an expensive one and I could hardly believe that I was about to get inside it. Eager to touch it and too eager to act like a gentleman, I dashed to the back doors of the car and held it open for the women to enter.I had a grin on my face, sure that this would impress Chioma, but she did not even look remotely moved by my gesture. I sat in the front with the driver and as soon as I closed my door, we were off.

"Sorry, we are dropping them at home first" I said to the driver.

"Ok sir, where do they live?"

"Sorry ladies, what is your address?" Chioma leaned forward and addressed the driver.

"Oh, do you know General Linus' house, in Eko estate?"

"Yes ma, I know where General Linus lives."

The car was silent for a while, then the driver leaned over and switched on the radio. There is something magical about being driven at night with afrobeats playing and the air conditioning blasting out.

"So Chioma," I began, looking straight ahead, "you said earlier that you have to go to the hospital tomorrow morning, I hope you are ok?"

"Oh yeah," she laughed "I am a medical student so when I am home, I try and get a few hours of practice in and do what I can. "

"Wow, so what do you want to specialise in, do you know yet?"

"Yeah, right now, I'm leaning towards gynaecology. I want to be able to help other women."

"That's so admirable. I wish I could help people."

"Oh, what do you do George?"

"I'm, uh, trying to be an investment banker. But I currently am not working at a firm, soon though, hopefully."

"I hear investment banking is extremely stressful."

"Hana, nowhere near as stressful as medicine." She laughed. "And you Lulu," trying not to be rude, I asked, "What do you do?"

Lulu had been on her phone, barely paying us any attention.

"Engineering, mechanical," she said.

"Oh forgive Lulu," Chioma added, "She's had quite a bit to drink. She's not normally this quiet."

"Oh," I laughed, I wasn't interested in talking to her anyway "so your father is a general, that sounds interesting."

"Well yeah, he used to be, nowadays he just does a lot of business and politics like most of the men here. Very non-descript, very informal. What do you parents do?"

"Well, in all honesty, I don't know. I don't actually know who my biological parents are. I was raised by estranged family in Belgium."

"Wow, that must have been difficult for you."

"At times, but they loved me a lot so I was very lucky growing up."

"That's nice. Anyway, what brought you to Africa anyway?"

" Well I have always been interested in Africa, and I had a couple African friends when I was in university, Ohi and Folusho, and they were the ones who always insisted on me visiting so, here I am I guess."

Time had really flown by because we started to veer off the road and pull into her estate

"Oh, that's nice. Well here we are, the second house on the right is my stop. It was nice meeting you George, well, since you are friends with my brother, I'm sure I'll see you around. Come on Lulu, let's go."

"Ok, I'll see you soon. Have a good night."

She and Lulu came out the car and even as we were driving away, I couldn't take my eyes off her, until she disappeared inside the house. Wow.

I eventually got to Alhaji's house, he only lived about 15 minutes away from Chioma. His house was unsurprisingly huge, with steps leading up to a portico supported by Corinthian pillars. The whole aesthetic was white and monochrome, with plenty of greenery and glass. Alhaji was definitely someone who had wealth and knew how to spend it. When I entered the house, none of the family was awake but a maid directed me to the room I was supposed to be staying in. She said that Alhaji and his wife would like to have breakfast with me at 10am sharp. It was only when she left the room that I was able to take it all in. I felt like I was in a different world, one with flat screen televisions embedded on the walls and beds that could fit ten people comfortably. I felt awkward and embarrassed getting into the bed because I felt like

I could lie all I want when I am awake, but somehow, my dreams would betray. Nevertheless, I was exhausted. I thought about Officer and Aunty Gloria, I thought about Folusho and grandma, I thought about the image of my mother's face, and then finally, I thought about Chioma. Then I fell asleep.

9

The dining room was full of so much natural light that I wasn't sure if all the food laid out on the long-stretching table was even real or simply a mirage. Eggs three ways, sausages, bacon, baked beans, tomatoes, five different types of cereal excluding porridge and muesli, yoghurt, bread baskets, and of course, yam and corned beef stew, akara and pap, a fruit bowl as well as a vibrant fruit salad, fresh juices and smoothies.

"George, you must try one of the croissants and tell me if they are as good as you have them back home" said Alhaji's wife, Halima. Even at 10am she was an extremely glamorous woman, dressed in loose fitting white linen and with hair sleeked stylishly to the back. Despite drinking her ginger tea from porcelain white china, her immaculate red lipstick was not disturbed. I complemented Halima on the exquisite array of food and tried the croissant.

"So what are your plans for today George?" Alhaji asked, all the way from the head of the table as he reached for the fish stew to accompany his third piece of yam.

"Actually, I am going to The Pavillion later on, Uti, uh, General Linus' son invited me to come and have lunch with him and a couple of his friends. I met them yesterday at the wedding."

"Interesting. Very good, I know General Linus well. Actually, I was hoping to meet with you tonight, but I have some work to do with Kwame Doso so I will most likely be home late. In fact, I will be busy with Kwame for the rest of the week."

"Kwame?" exclaimed Halima "I thought he was still in Saudi Arabia."

"Yes, he only just flew back last night. Something came up," answered Alhaji "Anyway, will you be available next Monday? I have been thinking about what we discussed yesterday and there is something I think might interest you."

"Of course, I don't have anything planned for then."

At breakfast I met Alhaji's sons, Yakubu and Abu. Yakubu was 19, second year law student at Oxford university, and Abu was 13, he went to boarding school in England, Halima said that hopefully he would grow up to become an accountant but for now, only football interested him. They seemed like nice boys, or perhaps just disinterested, either way, they were quiet. Abu was clearly the extrovert of the two them, after breakfast, he came to my room to show me photos of him playing football and the prizes he had won. Alhaji had an older daughter as well but Halima said that she worked and lived for the most part in New York. I wasn't really told much more about her than that.

I spent the rest of the afternoon sat in the garden, thinking about how far I had gotten. I couldn't afford to get comfortable, after all, I was still very much disposable to these people. I also had to get a firm grip on all the lies I had told them so far. Just like Folusho had predicted, George Peterson was being embraced with open arms, our plan was working.

When it was about 3, the driver from yesterday, Kunle, drove me down to The Pavilion. Alhaji had assigned him to me for the duration of my stay, which was beyond ideal. I walked into the restaurant, which was more of a lounge, and asked to be directed to the waterfront. As expected, Uti was not there yet. While I waited for him, I decided that it was the perfect opportunity to update Folusho on everything that had happened and let him know that I was ok. Just as I had sent the message and put the phone down, Uti had appeared, along with three other guys. I got up upon seeing them and greeted them with the customary informal sloppy handshake that guys do.

"I hope you haven't been waiting here long, we Africans operate under a different time zone I'm afraid" Uti joked "Anyway, I don't know if you remember these guys from last night; TK, Julius and Ireti, my childhood friends."

"So do you guys usually come here?" I asked

"Yeah, well I guess you can say that. We go to all the good places in the zone, and sometimes, in the One zones."

"But sometimes, we find the One zones too rough and crowded so we tend to just stay here" added TK.

"Oh okay, I only really passed through a One zone on the drive here, I didn't really see what it was like in all honesty" I said.

"Oh don't worry, there isn't really much beyond these borders" replied Uti.

We enjoyed a few drinks in the open air. The waterfront was basically a series of cabanas facing the water, it was nice. There was a football match on so fortunately, I didn't have to put on my persona, I was free to just enjoy the game as Kanmi. Arsenal lost 5-1 at home to Bayern Munich. I learnt that Uti and Julius were Arsenal fans because after the match, they became very sober and quiet, and as a result, very drunk and loud. By the amount of beers they were drinking, you would think they were trying to drown the individual sorrows of every member of the team. TK found it particularly hilarious.After some more pitiful lounging, Uti decided that the best way to get over his sadness was to go out clubbing later on that night. He asked me if I would like to come with them but I gracefully declined, I didn't think it would be respectful to Alhaji to go out in the middle of the night. However, I did agree to come and play football with them on Thursday morning.

I got home around 8:30 and the house was quiet as ever. I went into my room, the sheets had been changed and my clothes had been arranged into the wardrobe. I sat in the armchair and suddenly realized that I had not checked my phone to see if Folusho had replied. He had.

"Be careful."

The rest of the week featured many of the same sorts of things. There was a lot of food, always. I saw more of Uti and his friends, after the match on Thursday morning, we went to a penthouse owned by Uti's dad. The whole place deceitfully antique looking, with many chrome touches and trendy appliances installed for that modern twist. The fridges were fully stocked with Grey Goose bottles and Belvedere, that finding water was a rarity. On the weekend, he invited me down to a polo club to watch his friend Femi play a championship game. The funny thing was that we didn't get to the club until after the game was finished so we just stayed for the after party.I even went to his family home one evening to play some FIFA with the boys. After I lost tragically to TK, seeing as I had never played the game before, I decided to go and sit in the main room until it was my turn to play again. As I was composing a quick text to Folusho on my phone, I heard footsteps coming my way. I quickly stood up, fearing that it might be Uti's father, General Linus, who I had not yet met. It was Chioma. She looked more surprised to see me than I did her, yet she met me with the most beautiful smile.

"Hi, George right? What are you doing here?"

"Hey, actually, your brother invited me. We have been hanging out all week."

"Ah, I see. My condolences." She giggled. I laughed way too much at this, awkwardly so.

"Anyway, how have you been?" I asked, now looking down at my shoes in embarrassment.

"I've been alright, the hospital has been less stressful than usual this week, which is a good thing I guess."

"That's nice to hear" I remarked, scratching my arm. Great, she is going to think I have dry skin.

"Well, what have you been doing with my brother? I hope he is showing you other things besides getting drunk." I laughed again, this time too quietly, making a conscious effort not to embarrass myself again, even though I think that was equally as bad.

"Well yeah, I've been having a really good time. We even

just went to watch a polo match, which is something I have never done before. But I would like to see what the food is like around here before I go. Is there anywhere you would recommend?"

She smiled and moved a little closer to me. "Well, there is this new place called 'Tutu's Jasmine' which my friends keep telling me is really good, but I haven't been."

I inhaled deeply. "Well, since you haven't been, why don't we go there together, I mean, if you want to." I started scratching my head now, immediately regretting what I had just done. My spirit was clenching unto my chest, already dreading her response.

"Yeah, I'd like that. How does Wednesday evening sound? 7:30?" I exhaled.

"Perfect, Wednesday it is." Just at that moment, Uti came into the room. After looking at Chioma and I suspiciously, he said,

"Guy, its your turn o."

At that I just smiled weakly at her and pointed towards Uti's room and started walking away. I didn't even say goodbye. Oh well, I was seeing her soon.

Alhaji's office was very much like him, very big, full of expensive things, desperate to look like a showroom from Architectural Digest. His meeting was running late so he asked Kunle to bring me so he could finally show me what it was he wanted to show me. I had no idea what this thing could be but I really couldn't say no to him. Right behind him hung his own portrait, as if that wasn't narcissistic enough, it looked as if the image had been altered to show Alhaji as he sees himself: sharper, more chiselled, with more masculine features.

"Ah, George, welcome. Take a seat."

Once I had sat down, he pulled out an old leather-bound book from inside the top drawer of his huge distressed oak desk. There was something poacher-esque about him as he sat behind the desk, something illegal, something destructive. He smiled at me.

"Here, read this?"

"What is it?"

"Voltaire's treaties on the nature of humans. I very much enjoyed studying it when I was at university. What are your views on his ideas?"

"Um, I'm afraid I am not familiar with Voltaire."

"Ah, well you will be soon, don't worry. Open the book, can you read the inscription to me?"

The book was so tattered, it was obvious that it had been a favourite of Alhaji's. I held it delicately in my hand and turned the cover with the utmost care. Sure enough, the inscription was on the title page, it was in French.

"Go ahead George, what does it say?"

My mouth was dry. I didn't really expect anyone to challenge my charade.

"I uh.."

"You are not really from Belgium, are you?" I froze, I didn't know what would happen now. Alhaji laughed. "Its okay, do you really think I didn't know already?"

Huh? I was so confused.

"How? How did you know?" I asked, dumbfounded.

"It was quite simple actually. You were too quick to agree with me at the wedding. I asked you if you were an investment banker and if you had studied politics and you just went along with it without even giving as much as a story or something to make the charade more believable."

"So what happens now?"

"Nothing. I'm actually really glad that I met you George. To be totally honest with you, I know what you are. You see, you may look the part, but your eyes give you away, the way they move. I know that you are an albino" at this, an evil smile crawled across his face and he flashed his glistening teeth at me. "You see, George, there are a couple of projects I am working on and I could really do with some good luck."

"Alhaji, what are you trying to say?" I began to back away from him, even though he had not left his seat the entire time. Alhaji retrieved a necklace from within the same drawer the book had been in. The necklace had been beaded with what looked like many white beads or shells.

"My grandfather was a prolific albino hunter and he taught me how to spot albinos. When he died, he gave me this necklace, he told me it would bring good fortune to everything I laid my hands on, and he was right.Who would have known that there was so much power in just a handful of the teeth of an albino." He laughed again. "Now I have a whole one to myself."

I began to tremble. How did I not see this coming? Why did I not question his out of place kindness?

"Alhaji, please?"

"I already know what I want to do with your head, I will bury it in the garden of my house. Oh I am so happy, it's just a matter before all I have worked for comes into fruition. Once all the rituals are performed, I will have unparalleled power."

Just as he finished speaking, two men burst through the door, both wearing only black and either looking capable of much more than murder. Before I could even catch my breath, they had grabbed my arms and began carrying me out of the office. Could the other employees not hear? Where they not moved by this?

"Alhaji wait! Wait! I can help you!" Alhaji was not moved by my screams. "Wait! I know another way! I can make you the most powerful man in Africa!" He suddenly became interested.

"Stop" He said to the men. "What are you talking about?"

I closed my eyes and spent some time gathering myself.

"You see," I begun "the reason why I am here in the first place is because I am trying to get to the Capital. I have business with the Fathers."

"What business could you possibly have with them? Even if you manage to get into the Capital, they will just order you to be killed."

"Actually, no. If they wanted me dead, they will have killed me many years ago, the fact they kept me alive shows that I am important to them, however, they decided to banish me to the Wasteland which shows that they must see me as some sort of threat."

"Wait, what are you saying?"

"I'm saying that once I find out why they banished me, I will be able to leverage that and I can use it to get you the power that you want."

The Alhaji paused to think about my proposition. My heart was thumping so loudly through the tension filled room that I was convinced that they all could here it, nevertheless the men still held on to me as tightly as ever.

"I want my daughter Zara to marry the son of the Father of All. If you can make him marry her instead of that stupid Chief's daughter, I will let you live. If you cannot achieve this, I will not only sacrifice you, but I will also sacrifice your uncle and grandmother too, after all, I have already promised your legs and right arm to Kwame." I was shocked.

"How do you know about my family?" Alhaji grinned again.

"Young man, you seriously underestimate me. On this land, I am one of the most powerful men, both in the physical and spiritual. There is nothing I can't find out. Once I had gotten the footage of you getting dropped off at the hotel that day, it didn't take long for me to track down the car and indeed the owner of it. Unfortunately for you, that your uncle has a big mouth, according to my men, he had gone around informing people that he had found his long-lost nephew. It really wasn't that hard at all. Just make sure that your little plan works." The men released me at this point and Alhaji ushered them to leave the room. Alhaji picked up the pen on his desk and resumed his work. "You can leave now, Kunle will take you back home."

That night was one of the hardest nights of my life. Lying in a bed in the house of a man who I naively trusted, a man who was pure evil, I couldn't get to sleep. However, as the only hope I had of reaching the capital was through him, I was going to have to find a way to make it work. Moreover, the lives of my family were at stake, my family that I only just found out I had. I couldn't afford to fail. I wanted to call Folusho and tell him what had happened but something inside me prevented me from doing so. I didn't want to scare them like this. I just put the picture of my mother on my chest and pressed my eyelids as firmly as they would shut. I let the tears fall down my face and wet pillows until they carried me to sleep.

The days went by slowly now. I spent a lot of my time in the room, trying to interact with Alhaji's family as little as I could, to the point where Alhaji must have told them that I was sick because the maid brought me a basket full of different medications, tissues, blankets, a hot water bottle and a get well card signed from Halima. She was such a lovely woman, I wonder if she knew that she had really married a brute.

As much as I had lost my appetite those last couple of days, I didn't forget about my dinner plans with Chioma that Wednesday and come 7:15, I was dressed in my finest suit, ready to receive her at the restaurant. It was a nice place, very Afro-European, with authentic handcrafted furniture that were all mismatched, and very contemporary African art taking various mediums from pottery and painting to sculpture and song. It had very low lightening with crystal chandeliers and scented candles and there was a grand piano in the corner with a man playing the most delicate Afro-Jazz, accompanied occasionally by the sounds of a subtle saxophone harmony. It really was an experience, and Chioma looked absolutely stunning. She was wearing a silk black dress that just came off the shoulders and had her hair sleeked to the back. She said she was just coming from a function and didn't mean to be this overdressed, but I'm confident enough to say that she was all dressed up for me. The night was wonderful. We talked and drank and had the most delicious food, it was all traditional African food, but tasted like nothing I had ever had before. Chioma even asked me to go dance, and being the gentleman that I was, I obliged, but despite my new identity, even

George Peterson couldn't mask the terrible dancing of Adekanmi. As much as I enjoyed the evening, the only negative aspect of it for me was having to live a lie. There were so many times when we would be talking about something and I would so much want to tell her about my true life experiences or my true self, but I couldn't. I had to not be Kanmi and I had to be George. All of this made me think, who was it she liked? Did she like me for me or for the man I was pretending to be? Nevertheless, I didn't want to know the answer, I was just happy for her to like me either way.

The next couple of days were nice. Whenever Chioma had a free moment, we would do things like get ice cream in her lunch break or go to the cinema to watch a film, or even just going for a walk. It was sublime. However, she always made it clear that we were just friends and nothing more. To be honest, this hurt my feelings because I had never felt this way for anyone in my entire life. She said that she didn't want anything long distance and that inevitably, I would have to be leaving for Belgium soon. More importantly, she would often say sort of jokingly that she was only interested in being with someone who she could see herself marrying, and at the end of the day, her father would never allow her marry someone who was foreign. This point in particular really shook me because I assumed that since Africans loved and embraced foreigners so much, surely they would be thrilled at the prospect of a foreigner marrying into the family. Of course I had never heard of or seen interracial marriages, but foreigners never come beyond the Ones zone, plus, I had had an extremely limited experience of the world and of people so I couldn't really judge. I was very much aware of the tribalism that took place on the continent, I had learned of the Biafran war too. But I thought

into that building. Once you are in, you will have to make your way to the Pentagon."

"What is the Pentagon?"

"The room where the Fathers spend most of their time, discussing national and foreign affairs and whatnot. It is on the top floor of the building, right in the centre. Actually, forget it, you will never be able to make it there, the security in the building is incredibly tight. I will have to think of something else."

"Alhaji, don't worry, just get me in, I will find a way."

The next couple of days were spent in preparation to go to the Capital. Passport pictures were taken, documents were forged, even a real cameraman was hired to make the aesthetic look even more convincing. As soon as everything was ready, that evening, for the first time, Alhaji brought my new passport, my letter of employment and all the paperwork necessary to enter the Capital. Although it was all fake, it was all so realistic, everything to the fact that my working visa was sponsored by the British Broadcasting Cooperation amazed me. I was now a British journalist from the BBC here to enquire about the trade deal the Father of All, Akinrinnola Adegboyega, had signed during his official visit to Singapore. Alhaji wanted me to leave the next day but I asked him for one last day to get myself ready. The truth of the situation was that I really wanted to see Chioma one last time because I wasn't sure what my life was going to be like after I come back from the capital, or if indeed I would make it out at all. Either way, I would have no reason to stay in the Upper zone as if I did leave the capital alive but was unable to keep my promise to Alhaji, I would be a dead man anyway. In all honesty, I didn't really know how I could even keep my word to him, I knew that I had played up my importance to him, but what choice did I have? I needed to be alive, I needed my family to be alive. I had come too far and sacrificed too much to not even get to the capital, and now, my time had finally come.

10

The car journey to the border was brief but quiet. Kasim, the cameraman, drove while I sat impatiently in the passenger's seat. I was trying to act calmly but I couldn't help squeezing the sides of my chair the whole time. At first, he was asking me a lot of technical questions about how I wanted him to shoot but of course, I know nothing about being a journalist so I just joked and said that whatever makes me look good. Eventually, he resulted to putting on the radio but because it was still so early in the morning, about 5:30, there wasn't really anything playing. It was interesting to see how, unlike in the other zones where the streets were very busy at this time, here, there was virtually no one about. I guess sleep really is only for those who can afford it.

We pulled up to the border and this border was very different to the other ones. There was a single lane, I guess, for people who had been granted access, and a separate gate only for the Fathers.

The gate for the fathers didn't have any security checkpoints, only a guard at a booth stationed to open the gate whenever they were passing through. However, our lane first had a tunnel which we had to drive through, which, I was told, did a 360 scan of the contents of the car. Then an official came through with some sort of detector to sweep the car through. Finally, we reached the biometrics and paperwork stage. The official taking our details in seemed to know Kasim quite well, which was explained by the fact that his fingerprints were already in the system. It turns out, Kasim was a regular at these press conferences, an old hand at filming. He even said that he had wanted to be a movie director but, as a Middle, he didn't have enough money to go to film school so he just settled for this and it had done him well. When it was my turn to be processed through, I got extremely nervous. The security at this border was so high-tech, there was no way that I could get away with this. Just as my fears were escalating, the official looked up to me and motioned for me to come closer to him. As I walked towards, I could feel every fibre in my limbs trembling.

"Oga, where are you from?" he asked, with a cheeky smile on his face.

"What do you mean? Do you not see my passport?"

"Answer the question first now, ah ah. Obey before complain o."

"I am George Edwards, a British citizen." I said, with all the conviction and irritation I could muster.

"Okay, oga Mr Edwards, if you want to pass to this place, you must first settle us."

I was only to eager to do this. Within minutes, I had given them all the cash that I had, we had collected our visitors' passes and were on our way to Aso Rock Hill.

The Capital was very different from what I had imagined. There was only one straight road divided into two lanes by an extremely neat median strip. That was probably the only contained greenery because on both sides were great big palm trees with looming branches towering above the car. Equally, it was fair to say that the flags on display outnumbered the people by ten. There were giant flag-poles waving all the flags of the old African countries before the PanAfrican reform. Flying on either side of the gate of Aso Rock Hill was the new African flag. The new flag had the colours; red, black, yellow and green in blocks horizontally across, with the images of a lion, an eagle, a stallion, a serpent and an elephant to represent each ancestral forefather. Once our visitors' passes had been checked and our biometrics had been taken again, we were directed to press parking. We climbed the great steps to enter the ornate building, and Kasim showed me the way to the pressroom. After about half an hour of setting up, the press conference begun. A young looking man, mid thirties, stood behind the podium with the official seal and presented all the announcements he had for that day. At first, I contemplated sneaking out of the conference to find the Pentagon, but then I noticed that two security personnel manned the door so I thought it best to stay until the end. Fortunately for me, I didn't really have to do anything; the other reporters were itching to probe the man for more information so I just had to sit and look interested.

Eventually, the conference came to an end and we were given an hour to vacate the premises. As Kasim was packing up his equipment and beginning to head outside to pack it up in his boot, I sat down, pretending to make notes. When he came back and asked if I was ready to go, I told him that he could wait for me in the car, I just needed to finish this quickly. Accordingly, he left, and as the room began to empty out with just a couple of reporters left, also making notes, the two guards left the doors and went somewhere else. This was it, this was my chance. I walked out of the room, and as Alhaji had told me, I began looking for a means to get upstairs. I saw an elevator, but I knew that there would be more attention there and I would be more likely to be seen if I took it, so I checked to see if there were some stairs somewhere. I did find the stairs. The stairs were behind a brown door so they were not so obvious, but there was a glass panel in the door, which let me, see them. They were black marble and had wooden banisters on the side. They were in the corner of the building and were just the typical revolving 'L' shaped stairs so I assumed they were service stairs, which was perfect for me. I ran up the stairs all the way to the top and as luck would have it, I managed not to run into anyone. However, as soon as I stepped through the doors at the top of the stairs to enter the rest of the floor, I could see that a woman was sat at a desk a couple of feet away. Her desk was one of those high ones that only let you see her face, but I could tell that she was not a pleasant person. Her dress matched her old grey hair and she had tied her hair up in a bun that looked like it was pulling the blood vessels in her eyes up too.

"Can I help you?" she asked, with a forced smile on her face.

"Yes, actually, I am here from the BBC. I have an 11:30 appointment. I was told to come to the Pentagon." I was shaking. I could feel the sweat buds forming on my brow and dripping down my collar.

"Please have a seat, let me just verify." She got up and

motioned for me to sit in the chairs in the indent of the elevators, which was decorated like a little lounge area, complete with a little coffee table and varying freshly printed newspapers. As she started making her way to the Pentagon to verify what I had said, I began to panic, I knew that once she realised that I was lying, security would immediately be called and that would be the end of me. I decided to follow her, silently so she wouldn't notice. I stayed far enough away at first, fortunately, the floors were carpeted with this deep crimson that matched the intensity of the mahogany walls. All down the corridor I could see portraits of men I assumed to be past Fathers, all looking imperial and somewhat voyeuristic. As she got closer and closer to this great double doors, I began to shorten the distance between us, and as soon as she pushed the door open, I pushed past her and threw myself into the midst of 5 confused men. Before I knew it, I could feel hands all over me. Security had already begun to pile on top of me and I knew that the next few seconds were critical.

"Wait," said a robust voice, coming from the man seating at the head of the table. He was dressed in a black buba and sokoto with a cap that looked like that of a Fulani man. "Who are you?"

"My name is Adekanmi. I have come a very long way to see you all and before they take me away, please, let me ask only two questions."

"Take him away jo" scoffed another man, one of the two I had seen at the wedding that day.

"Yes, go and deal with him" shouted another man, speaking with a Hausa accent.

"No," bellowed the man in black, and at his word, the others were pacified"Young man, ask your questions."

The guards released their grip on me but their heavy presence was still very much felt. I reached within my blazer pocket and at that, I was immediately pushed to the ground by a guard.

"Its okay" said the man in black "allow him retrieve what he has"

I got back up and put my hands in the air.

"It's just a picture, I swear. If you don't believe me, you can reach for it yourself."

Indeed, the guards did not believe me and one of them slowly reached for within my pocket and brought the picture out.

"Please," I continued, "open it up"

The guard opened it and showed it to the Fathers.

"My Fathers, do any of you recognise this woman?"

"Akinrinnola, why are you allowing this boy to waste our time like this?"

said the other man that I recognised from the wedding.

"Yes, what is our business with a girl like this? I will not tolerate this embarrassment" said the one with the Hausa accent who had spoke before.

"Bring the picture to me" ordered the man in black, who it was clear was the Father of All. The guard holding the picture rushed over to give it to him and bowed as he presented it. "Boy, who is this woman and how do you know her?"

"This is my mother. She has been missing for 23 years. "

"Do you know how many people go missing everyday? Why would you think we know her" shouted the last man, who had not spoken yet, an Edo man.

"Wait, Efeosa, this is not a time for anger. But young man, he is right, why should we know her?"

"Because, Fathers, I believe you were involved. I know for a fact that it was you who gave the orders for me to be banished to the North Wasteland and grow up not knowing anything about myself and I want to know why."

"Akinrinnola, please, let them take this boy away, he is just annoying me. Ah ah, what is it? Boy, how dare you talk to your elders like this?" the Edo man was now standing up and looking at me with one eye squinted and his lip raised, like a bull about to charge at the red.

"I've already told you Efeosa, relax. This is a matter that concerns me." At this the Father of All stood picking up his walking stick, the silver lion's head on the top of the cane gleamed as the light touched it. He clenched the head and slowly, made his way to me. I had seen him before, on television and in newspapers, he looked much healthier, much younger, with more strength, but now I could see that he was even struggling to walk. His age really had taken its toll on him. He eventually got to me and looking me in the eyes, said "Young man, I am the one who sent you away and I'll tell you why. That woman is your mother, many years ago, she used to look after the children of my good friend, Late Charles Ubong. We used to always laugh about how fresh she was. One day, I asked him to send her to my house to collect a package for him, and, lets just say she got something a little different from what she was expecting. Now, as soon as I realised she had fallen pregnant, it was too late, she was already far-gone. The girl didn't say anything until it was already obvious, then she went to Charles' wife Stephanie to confess what had happened. I mean, I wasn't too bothered by the whole thing, it wasn't the first time that another woman had fallen pregnant for me. So I did what I always do, I bought her a house in some middle zone or two zone, and the plan was to kill her and the baby as soon as it was born. But as soon as I got wind of what you were, I couldn't bring myself to kill you. I asked the man who killed your mother to bring you to me so I could see you. I remember, your skin, it was so cold, so pale. That was when I was convinced you had to live. You were different. However, I knew what people would say if they found out that I, Akinrinnola Adegboyega, fathered a cold one, I couldn't have it. So that's why I had to send you away."

In that moment, I felt weightless. I felt like I had left my body and was only listening in on what was going on. I was in utter disbelief. What kind of narcissistic hedonistic monster of a man is this? He raped and killed my mother. He raped and killed several other woman and children. To be honest, looking at all of these men, they probably are just like him. Is that what power does? I really didn't know how to react, I knew I came here for answers but what I had discovered was more than I could comprehend.

"So you are my father?" I whispered. He stretched out his hand and grabbed my shoulder.

"You are my son."

The other four fathers were in shock, one covered his mouths with his hand as if to retain whatever foul words he had in his head, the Edo man removed his cap and placed both hands on his shiny head as if in agony, from the two men from the wedding; one of them had put his hand on his head and his elbow against the table, looking at the ground with his head tilted at an angle, the other sat with his back against the chair and his two hands just hanging lifelessly downwards, with his head facing the glass ceiling. Even the guards had backed away at this point, unsure about what to do.

"Adekanmi, the truth is that ever since I sent you away, I used to see you in my dreams sometimes. In fact, there is this recurring dream I have of a cold boy like you, with hair, wild like a lion's mane, he is dressed in all white. The boy is standing at the top of a great staircase while I wait at the bottom. In my dream, I always see the boy jump from the top of the staircase and every time, I see myself catch the boy as he falls. In fact, I am not surprised to see you at all, I always knew that one day, I would see you again when the time was right."

As he was saying all of this, I didn't know how to feel. Was I supposed to be angry with him, for everything that he has done to me and my family, was I supposed to be happy that I know the truth now and that I have a father, what was I supposed to feel?

He led me to his office to discuss things further without the dumbfounded gaze of the audience of the Pentagon. I sat in the chair opposite his desk and he sat in the seat beside me instead of his own behind the desk.

"Adekanmi, listen to me. I am dying. I have been seating in this office, ruling this continent for over 30 years now and my body is failing me. I cannot do the work for much longer. Currently, my son Tofarati, who is probably about ten years older than you is supposed to take over from me. But you are my son too, and before I die, I want to make peace with you. I am offering you the chance to be the next Father of All, Adekanmi, that is, if you want it."

"But sir, I am so young, I am nobody." I said, trembling at the very prospect.

"Be quiet. You are not a nobody. You are an Adegboyaga, do you know what that means? Your bloodline has ruled this great continent for years. You are royalty on this land."

"But what about my skin? People will never accept me as their leader?"

"Look, times are changing. If you are the Father of All, they will have no choice but to accept you."

"What about your other son, he has been expecting this all his life."

"Don't worry about that, leave him to me."

"Sir, I…" I began shaking my head.

"Just consider it."

The next couple of days were incredibly fast paced. I was put up in the official state guesthouse, which was the only house in the Capital that didn't belong to a Father. Over the next couple of days, my father introduced me to the rest of his family. He and his wife Niyoola had two children, a son and daughter, both older than me, and I spent a lot of time with them according to his request. It was easy for me to feel the waxiness of their reception to me, I could feel Niyoola and Tofarati burning holes through me with their stares when I wasn't looking. He insisted that I eat dinner with them as a family and that I accompany him to all his official functions. By the end of the week, a press conference was held on my behalf and I was formally introduced to the world as his son. Even as I stood there, shaking hands with all the Fathers in front of a thousand snapping cameras, even then, I was met with a grip too hard or a pat on the back too aggressive to suggest a happy union. At first, the reception of the public was good, but then news started to spread of riots in some of the outer zones. My father was laughing about this, saying that they were "uncivilised pigs anyway" but that didn't console me. I would occasionally hear the Fathers or their staff make a derogatory comment about me or even say something to me in passing. Acceptance clearly wasn't just a problem for the uncultured.

One day, I was in the Upper zone with father, attending some birthday party for his friend. I was still getting used to the attention, smiling when you were supposed to smile, having endless casual conversations with people who wanted to act like they had known you all their lives. Tofarati was an expert. He moved around the crowd so seamlessly. When I sat down at an empty table somewhere in the back of the room, having finally decided to take a break from all the socialising and networking, the most amazing thing happened. I felt a tap on my shoulder, only to turn around and see that it was Chioma. I sprung up immediately and gave her the tightest hug.

"Chioma, its so good to see you how have you been?"

"Me, I should be the one asking you, Adekanmi." I froze.

"Oh, you heard."

"How wouldn't I hear? The world has heard. Why didn't you tell me?"

"I, I couldn't. I didn't know. I didn't like lying to you, not once, but I didn't have a choice, I'm sorry."

"Its okay. I can understand."

"Well, now that you know who I am, do you still want to hang out sometime?"

"How does Friday night sound?"

"It sounds good."

Alhaji also made sure that I wouldn't forget about my promise to him. Folusho told me that he had sent a group of thugs to their house in the middle of the night to completely destroy his taxi and steal whatever they could get their hands on from the house. Folusho had been instructed to pass the message on to me, that I would understand. I got it loud and clear. First of all, it gave me an excuse to move the family to a nicer house. My father gave me the money to buy them a house in a One zone, where at least, there would be better security. In the meantime, I did try and do good on my word. I didn't know how to approach Tofarati about it so I just out-right told him the truth. He laughed at me. His wedding was already approaching and he had no desire to cancel it anyway, especially not for the benefit of a blackmailing thug. I begged and begged him but he said it was none of his concern. I knew better than to get our father involved, so I summed up the courage to go and see Alhaji myself the night before Tofarati's traditional wedding. I arranged to meet with him in his office, seeing as that was where the deal was made in the first place. I had never been there at night, it seemed much more terrifying, except this time, I had my own personal envoy so I knew that I was safe, but then again, it was Alhaji I was dealing with, he was a man capable of anything.

"Good evening Alhajji"

"So you have remembered me today Adekanmi. I hope you have some good news for me."

"Well, actually, I'm afraid not. I promise you, I tried everything to get Tofarati to marry Zara but he just refuses adamantly. He doesn't even love his fiancée. He doesn't care for her at all in fact. All he is concerned about is his public image and he says that cancelling the marriage at such a late stage will make him look very unserious, besides, he doesn't see anything for him to gain by marrying Zara anyway. "

"In other words, you didn't keep your promise to me, after everything I have done for you."

"Well, wait a minute sir. Actually, one of the other Fathers, Taiwo Famiyesin has a son, Dolapo, who is of marriageable age. He is still a bachelor and is looking for a woman to settle down with. Let Zara marry him instead. She will still give birth to a son to rule the continent. You will still get the power you desire, I can assure you."

"Kanmi, look, I don't want Dolapo. But as of now, I know what I want."

"What do you want Alhaji? Tell me."

"I know you are scared of me, and you have a right to be, but just remember, no matter how many men you pay to protect you, I can just as easily get to you and your family. What? You thought I didn't know that you relocated them? They are even closer to me now." Alhaji laughed sinisterly.

"Alhaji, what do you want."

"It's not time yet, when I'm ready, I'll tell you. But don't fail me again. I wont be so forgiving next time."

I left Alhaji's office and I didn't look back, at least I was free of him for now anyway. The next couple of months were bliss. I was free to see my family whenever I wanted, I would occasionally even drive down to see Officer. I even offered to give him some money or to help him with things as a means of saying thank you for all that he had done for me in my life but he vehemently refused, he liked the simple life and I respected that. I even tried to find Ohi again, I looked for him all over that Two zone and the Two zones that were near it, I even asked the woman who he used to deliver vegetables to, but no one knew where he had gone to. It was a shame. Best of all, over those last few months, things had really picked up between Chioma and I. Her father had finally given me his permission to date her, I suppose being the son of the Father off All can make a man overlook certain aspects. Things had gotten rather serious between us, yet it still felt like we didn't take ourselves so seriously, it was perfect. I even still hung out with Uti and TK and the boys from time to time. My life was the best it had ever been. I had friends, a family, and someone who loved me. I still had to live in the guesthouse in Capital because my father wanted me near him, but I didn't mind, it felt like a castle compared to everything I had ever lived in. I literally came from rags to riches, from a prison to a palace. I was blessed.

After some time, my father called me to come to his house to have a very important conversation. I could tell that this particular conversation was going to be different because there was something quite sombre about the atmosphere. When I got to his study in his house, I saw Tofarati already sitting in front of him, he was bent over with his head almost between his knees.

"Ah, Adekanmi, take a seat." Said my father. His voice was so weak, so frail, it sounded more like a shadow than a sound.

I went to the seat beside Tofarati and my eyes were fixed on him, I had never seen him lack composure before, not to talk of to this extent. Whatever was going on, it had to be really really bad.

"Adekanmi, I was just discussing with your brother here about my plans for the future. How I want things to be for when I move on."

"Sir, what are you talking about?"

"Remember that day you came, what I asked you?"

"Yes, I remember."

"Well, I need to know what you want to do. I have already informed Tofarati about it." He grabbed my hand "Adekanmi, I have done so much wrong by you. I want to make it right. I believe that those dreams that I had were for a reason. You are destined to be my successor."

"Father, but I am so young, how can I be the Father of All now? I don't know how to rule."

"Its okay, we can make you a Father now, and then make one of the existing Fathers the Father of All, then on your 35th birthday, you can take your rightful place as the lion of this great continent. That is just over 10 years away."

"But what about Tofarati? What will he do? He is just about to turn 35, it should be his turn to rule." Even as we were discussing him, Tofarati remained motionless, not even making a single sound. The shattering of his heart could be felt from miles away.

"Tofarati understands, we have already discussed it. I have made alternative plans for him. So son, what do you say? Honour the wish of a dying man and accept my proposal." At this, he squeezed my hand even tighter than before. I looked at him dead in the eyes, his eyes had sunken with the burden of a life long lived and a fire about to be extinguished.

"Okay father, I accept."

"Good. Your words bring so much joy to my ears. I have set up a little ceremony to announce this plan to the continent. It will be broadcasted at the end of the month, live from the steps of Aso Rock Hill. The reason why it needs to be done so soon is because I don't want the public to see me any worse than I am right now, I want them to remember me as I was in my prime and my condition is worsening by the day."

"Okay father, that is fine."

"Also, Adekanmi, I need to ask you something personal."

"What is it father?"

"How do you feel about this Chioma, General Linus' girl? I've been told of the way you two spend so much time together. Do you love her?"

"I do father."

"Can you see yourself marrying her?"

"I think so"

"Good. Well, you see, I know that you are still very young, very very young, but for the occasion, I need you to present her as your fiancé, even though you people are not engaged yet. Or even if you did decide to propose to her, there would be no need to have the wedding immediately, you might decide to prolong your engagement for several years until the both of you feel mature enough to get married, or even if you did decide to break of your engagement and get married to someone else later on. You see, the reason why it is so important for you to get engaged before the date, or at least, to lie and say you are engaged, is because the African people will accept you more as their future leader if you look like a man, and marriage is a way of affirming that masculinity because it suggests responsibility, accountability, compassion, commitment and all such qualities. Tofarati will be there with his wife as well that day so it only makes sense for you to have your woman by your side in public too. Do you see what I am saying, son?"

"Good. So talk to Chioma and let me know what she says."

The following weekend, I met with Chioma and told her everything my father had said. I explained to her how I was to be the next Father of All and how I had to wait until I was 35 to take on that office, I told her about the ceremony that was scheduled for two weeks time, and most importantly, I told her about how I wanted her there, as my fiancé. She was a little taken aback; she had only just become my girlfriend. But after I explained that we didn't have to get married straightaway and that there was still room for us to separate if things didn't work out, then she was more relaxed about the situation.

"Adekanmi, you are the most loving, humble and compassionate man I have ever met, but if you want to be engaged to me, you have to propose correctly." I laughed at this, and immediately got down on one knee to do the decent thing. That evening, we went to meet her father, General Linus, to explain the situation, and he was very comfortable with it all, "After all" he said, "it is usual for medical students to get engaged before they graduate anyway."

After a couple of days, word got around about my engagement and everywhere I went, I was being congratulated by well-wishers. So when I got a message that Alhaji wanted to see me, I assumed that he too just wanted to pass on his congratulations. He invited me back to his house to come and have dinner with his family since it had been such a long time since I had been there. It was at dinner that I met Zara for the first time. She had taken some time off work to spend with her family. She seemed like a pleasant girl, with her mother's looks and her father's stature. I didn't really think too much about her, but the work she was doing in New

York seemed really interesting. After dinner, Alhaji asked me to come and have a word with him in his car. This sounded odd to me but nevertheless, I obliged.

"So, Kanmi, you may not have realised this yet but the reason why I actually invited you here today is because I am ready to redeem my favour with you. In case you have forgotten, you owe me." I laughed.

"Don't worry Alhaji, I have not forgotten."

"Well, General Linus, carried away by his excitement, told me all about how you were going to be announced as the next Father of All which is why you proposed to his daughter so soon, so that you could parade your union to the world at the ceremony."

"Well, the announcement was supposed to be a secret, but seeing as you already know, I can't deny it."

"Good. Well, Adekanmi, I know what I want now."

"What is that?"

"I want you to announce my daughter, Zara, as your bride." I was stunned.

"Alhaji, I…"

"And if you don't, well, you already know what the forfeit is."

"Alhaji, no."

"I think you should go now. The ceremony is only a week away. There is probably a lot you should be attending to. I'll tell Halima that you had a wonderful time."

Just as he said that, he tapped on the window and the door on the side of the car that I was sitting on was opened for me. Unable to say anything, I just left the car and entered my own car to head home. My mind was completely blank. How was I going to fix this?

It was the morning of the ceremony. I was dressed in a white buba and sokoto and Chioma was wearing this beautiful emerald mermaid dress. We were stood on the right hand of my father. He was sat in his imperial blue buba and sokoto complete with his agbada and walking stick. On his left was Tofarati, who wore a grey buba and sokoto, and his new wife, who was wearing a blue nicely fitted iro and buba. The four other fathers were stood behind us, all wearing their traditional clothes too. The crowd at the bottom of the white marble steps was full of a collection of random people gathered from the different demes across the continent to make the ordeal seem more patriotic, as well as the ever-present press. The sky was blue, the flags were flying high, the air was fresh, the day couldn't be more picturesque. We had already had a little practice of the ceremony so I knew what I was supposed to do. My father was going to make a short speech, and then he would call me to the front of the steps to adorn me with the traditional symbols of the Father of All; a staff, some beads, a crown, and a loincloth. After that, I would take a seat in the chair next to him and drink palm wine from the cup he passed me. He would then invite Chioma to come and sit next to me and I was supposed to pass her the same cup so that she can drink from it too to join her to me. At that point, the crowds would cheer and Tofarati would lay his hand on my shoulder as a sign of support. Once all of that was done and we had posed for some pictures, I was supposed to ceremoniously lead the group into the Aso Rock building and the doors would be shut behind us. It was all quite straightforward. With just a few minutes to go before the service started, when we were already live on air, Tofarati walked over to my side and embraced me, knowing him, it was probably another PR stunt.

"You've taken this away from me" he said, in a very eerie manner "Just you wait."

I was confused, but very aware of the cameras so I just kept on smiling.

Then my father began his speech.

"Ladies and gentlemen on this great continent, young and old, today is a proud day to be African. Today, we are showing the world that we are a people who revere tradition and embrace progression. I have diligently served you all for 30 years of my life, and I am grateful for every morning and night that I get to do the work that I love so much. I love this continent with all my heart and best of all, I love the people of it. You all are what make Africa the sunshine of this world. You all are the reason that people have been fascinated for generations by our land and our culture. You all are the definition of strength, magic, fruitfulness and love. Every single one of you is an extraordinary creation, no matter what you look like, how dark your skin is, you are a gift from God. Therefore, it is a great thing for me to be able to share my joy with you. In my lifetime, I was fortunate enough to be blessed with these two sons, your sons. Today, I am dedicating them back to you. They will further the work that I have not yet finished, they will carry the load that I didn't yet pick up, and they will not cease until every stone is left unturned and they give you the Africa that our ancestors dreamt for us to have. Today, I am here to present to you my son, Adekanmi Adegboyega, as the future of this continent. He will be the next Father of All, he will be my successor, and through him, the traditions of this land will be fulfilled. I cannot hide the colour of his skin, and to those of you who have already expressed your sentiments on this matter, where you see that cold flesh, a warm eruption of blood flows through. He is just as African as every one of you, and I urge you to put your trust in him and support him just as you would support any other. It is now time for me to dress him in the adornments my own father dressed me in all those years ago."

At this, my father stood up, and led me to the front of the stage. Piece by piece he transformed me from the boy I knew well, to the man I now had to be.

"People of Africa, I now present to you your next leader, the tenth Father of All of this great Nation, Adekanmi Adegboyega. "

As I stretched out my hands as a sign of respect to the people, I felt the impact of something racing through me and I was on the ground in a matter of seconds. I didn't hear the sound until after I had already been hit and then the screams of the crowd was ringing in my ears. The entire place was in commotion, a state of frenzy, but there was nowhere to run to, the gates were still locked. I shut my eyes, trying to numb out the pain writhing in my body, trying to numb out every bit of the outside world. I was struggling to have any thoughts at this moment, all I could see was the face of my mother. I was angry with myself. I was in pain. I was tired.

"Kanmi. Kanmi." That was Chioma's voice. Her voice was pleasant, but it wasn't pleasant now. I opened my eyes to see her. She was draped over me, her emerald dress now sullied by my blood. "Don't go Kanmi, Just stay with me."

"I could see my father peering over me with tears in his eyes. I could see the other Fathers trying to console him. I could even see Tofarati's wife drenched with fear. I was tired of looking at them, so I closed my eyes again and looked back at my mother. I like her, and she likes me.